Azubike Okwudili Eze

Shadows of Yesterday

Contents

Subtle tones of eternity drowned in the murky waters of my pride and ego

My masquerading vanity made me immune to the thorns of unholy crown

The mask on my face entranced me with a macabre rhythm and lured me onto a lonely path coated with ephemeral colours

Tethering on the brink of darkness, I struggled to overpower the reasoning voice of my conscience

Oh despair! Please allow the light of my heart to kindle again

Who can help me? Who can save me from the dark shadows of yesterday?

1

The sky blazed cheerfully in tribute to nature's beneficence.

Bari King sat beside the driver, in the front seat of a shiny black and well-conditioned Toyota Corolla sedan. Dark sun glasses shaded his eyes, concealing any expression on his face, but the entire aura of his being was one of surefooted confidence. He glanced backwards at his convoy of eight similar vehicles and pursed his lips reassuringly. They drove fast and daringly away from Abonehma wharf and headed towards the intersection that led into the Old Government Reservation Area in Port-Harcourt. Pedestrians and motorists glanced at the convoy warily and hoped for the peace of the day to grow in vitality.

Few meters away from the intersection, Bari King pulled out his berretta M9 pistol and shot into the air. His men responded with their 7.62 mm Kalashnikov assault rifles, sending sporadic bursts piercing upwards through the air. The terror-stricken faces of pedestrians bore witness to the utter pandemonium that suddenly reigned on the road. Some of the footers fled into adjacent houses, while others with flawed articulation, ran paradoxically, headlong towards the oncoming convoy. Motorists reversed abruptly and escaped from the scene. Unlucky drivers who lost their nerves crashed their vehicles against electric poles and opposing automobiles. Armed policemen on duty at the intersection, desperate to save their lives, abandoned their rifles, truck and duty post, tearing away at their uniforms, as they fled.

They revealed the plain clothes they wore underneath, in case of such emergencies. As Bari King and his men maneuvered their vehicles into forces Avenue, Bari King released another round into the air, and his men backed him up with a chorus of rifle fire. The brazen assault on the peace of the neighbourhood replicated a similar pandemonium on the streets and prompted the residents to take cover in their homes and offices. The main gates of the State Headquarters of the State Security Services [SSS] were firmly locked, as they drove past it, hence the smooth ride they continued to enjoy. Bari King's mind was firmly focused on their target.

Upon sighting Old GRA Police station, Bari King retired his pistol to its holster and lifted his Israeli-made Uzi submachine gun. He adjusted the two belts of bullets which crisscrossed each other on his shoulders. The police check point, situated very close to the police station, was deserted as they passed it. They screeched to a halt in front of the police station, and Bari King alighted first from the vehicle. His gang of thirty-one men, with their shoulders similarly bedecked with crisscrossing chains of bullets, disembarked rapidly from their own vehicles. Approaching the locked gates of the police station, Bari King motioned to his men to remain still. His motions confident, Bari King shouldered his submachine gun and fired approximately 16 rounds of 9mm bullets through the gates of the police station, half emptying his magazine. Standing fearlessly in front of the badly damaged gates of the Police station, he failed to hear any deterring gunfire from the confines of the station. He beckoned his men, and they formed a semi-circle around him, with six men guarding the perimeter.

"We have buried fear in the forest of forbidden deaths and curses; we will charge in with a fury greater than that of a thousand hurricanes; are you with me?" hollered Bari King, without turning backwards.

"Ahoooaa" chorused his men, in a tone that portrayed fierce loyalty.

Bari King kicked in the gates and burst into the police premises. The fierce image he projected underscored the seriousness of his intentions. His men advanced behind him in a four row formation. The police station was silent and no policeman was in plain view. Bari signaled to his men to surround the bungalow that formed the administrative hub of the station, and they quickly fanned out and encircled it. He advanced towards the common hall, used for taking complaints and statements, with five of his men in tow. Alert and ready, they dashed into the hall through the unfastened door. Bari King's face was expressionless, as he observed the mass of uniformed and plainclothes police officers huddled together with some other civilians on the floor; they all lay face down on the floor, in a show of surrender. Pistols, rifles and shot guns were strewn about the floor, obviously abandoned by the policemen. Bari King instructed two of his men to gather the forsaken weapons and move them out of the hall. He veered away from the fainthearted policemen and moved, quickly, in the direction of the office of the Divisional Police Officer (DPO). Bari King kicked in the door of the office of the DPO and burst in with his men. Glancing about the office, he beheld an empty chair behind the desk. With cautious footsteps, he advanced towards the rear of the office, while the three men with him formed a rearguard. Sluggish movement behind the refrigerator caught his attention. Peering behind the refrigerator, he beheld the DPO cowering behind it. The bemused expression on his face guided his focus on the officer.

"Where are my men?" barked Bari King in an ominous tone, as

he pointed his weapon at the DPO.

His words jolted the DPO with fresh bolts of fright, and he crashed into the refrigerator. The Divisional Police Officer's slapstick act triggered gales of laughter from Bari King and his men.

"I hope you are not trying to play the comic with me; are you trying to provoke me further; I will blast you to tiny pieces and make you look uglier than minced meat, if you don't mind yourself" threatened Bari King, suddenly becoming serious.

The DPO awkwardly lifted himself up and nervously wiped his perspiring brow with the palm of his hand.

"Please follow me," mumbled the DPO as he made to leave his office.

"Wait there!" commanded Bari King, waving the DPO to stop.

The DPO stool still and stole uneasy glances at Bari King and his fierce looking men.

"Surrender your weapon now," dictated Bari King.

Conquering the short distance that separated him from his desk, the DPO pulled a lower drawer and retrieved his service revolver. With timorous motions he handed the gun to Bari King. Avoiding Bari King like a plague, he brushed the sides of his desk, as he proceeded away from his office. Bari King and his men, pointing four ominous guns at the DPO's rear outline, trailed after him as he approached a smaller outbuilding. The Divisional Police Officer's queasy legs failed him at the steps that led into the building and he crashed to the ground. Bari King's icy stare squeezed out life from the face of one of his men, who was about to break out in boisterous laughter.

"Will you get up and release my men now; you think I came here to watch your ill-conceived comic acts," intoned Bari King mercilessly.

The DPO wobbled to his feet and quickened his footsteps. A half – finished plate of rice on a disheveled table, soiled here and there by little rings and pools of coca-cola, greeted them as they entered an office. Reaching out to retrieve a key that hung on the wall, the DPO brushed against the table and sent the near-empty bottle of coca-cola crashing to the floor. The discordant sound emitted by the crashing bottle formed a belated and befitting symphony to the cowardly act of the fleeing policemen. The DPO unlocked a holding cell and four of Bari King's men sauntered out.

"Master!" hailed the formerly detained men, swinging their tightly clenched fists, in awe and respect, before Bari King.

Bari King's countenance was expressionless as he turned away from his men and focused his attention on the DPO.

"Open your armoury now!" barked Bari King.

The DPO hurried into the nearby office and retrieved another key. He sauntered to a steel door, an earshot away, and opened it. His head hanging low, he stood beside the door in a woebegone posture.

"Go and get all the guns and ammunitions," directed Bari King, waving his men forward without glancing backwards.

Obeying his instructions promptly, his men marched into the armoury and disposed it of its guns and ammunitions

"If you touch any of my men again, I'll turn the colours of your horizon into perpetual darkness," threatened Bari King, glaring hard at the DPO for a fleeting moment. Without emitting a sound, the DPO nodded acknowledgement. Waves of relief surged through him, instigated by the retreating footsteps of Bari King and his men.

Standing on the passageway that led into the main hall, Bari King waved his men out of the hall. The sudden sound of a heavy thud on the floor caused him to swing around abruptly, and he pointed his gun menacingly at the direction of the sound. He beheld one of his men quickly lifting himself from the floor and then placing the muzzle of his gun against the head of a prostrate policeman.

"What are you doing that for? Didn't you accidentally trip over him? I want to remind you that we are freedom fighters not killer's," cautioned Bari King.

With nimble footsteps, Bari King and his men trooped out of the police station. They entered their respective cars and sped off. The cache of arms that they dispossessed from the policemen swelled the contents of their booths. They drove into Aba Road and focused their attention on Eleme Junction. At Eleme Junction, they detoured to the right and journeyed along, unchallenged. Upon sighting the approaching convoy, the policemen stationed at intervening checkpoints along Refinery Road moved away from their positions with pretentious motions that masked their true fear. Awe and admiration oozed from the eyes of children, youths and a sprinkling of adults that lined the major road that led into Kino town, few kilometers from Bori town, as the convoy snaked through the barren road. The protruding stomachs of some of the children told many malnourished tales, and their torn clothes reeked of poverty. The fading colours of the clothes worn by most of the youths and adults betrayed their impoverished pockets.

"Slow down the vehicle; don't kick up so much dust; can't you see the people on the roadsides," directed Bari King in the lead vehicle.

The convoy maneuvered into the outlying grounds of a palatial mansion, and the armed guards closed the gate. Bari King and his men alighted from the vehicles with more relaxed bearings. They sauntered towards a canopy and took up positions on the steel- reinforced plastic chairs.

A bevy of young women, supporting some silver ware laden with pounded yam and native soup, promenaded towards Bari King and his men. Placing the container of food and plates before them, they began to dish it out. Generous quantities of fresh fish, dried fish, periwinkle and prawns steamed inside the plates, placed before the men. Their eyes glowed with bright expectations as they tackled the food. An assemblage of young men appeared with bottles of red wine, locally brewed gin, and hot drink and positioned them on the table.

After consuming his food and half bottle of red wine, Bari King stood up and a hush descended on his men.

"Mind how you drink; don't get drunk and lose your alertness," counseled Bari King in a commanding tone, as his roving gaze drew the attention of his men.

With his pistol firmly tucked away, Bari King ambled towards the main entrance of his tastefully finished mansion.

The sound of boisterous laughter from the midst of his men trailed after his medium-built frame. As few seconds separated him from the main door, it opened gently. Bari King stepped into the polished marbles of his foyer. Without batting an eyelid at the luxurious furnishing of his living room, he continued with unbroken strides along the staircase that led to his bedroom. As he approached the door of his bedroom, it opened and closed gently after him.

With growing ease, Nengi rose up from the bed and hurried towards Bari King. A poignant light danced inside her eyes, as she embraced him. In the same measure, Bari King responded with warm gestures of his own. Nengi's jean bum-shorts accentuated her proportionate and shapely lower frame, and her light skin flashed through the cleavage revealed by her deep-cut spaghetti blouse. Her long braids fell on her shoulders and framed the beautiful symmetry of her face. At five foot eight inches, she was slightly taller than Bari King.

"I'm glad to see you," stated Nengi, as she gazed into Bari King's eyes with a tender smile.

"Knowing that you're home, waiting for me, makes the whole load more bearable," replied Bari King in a softened tone.

"Do you still want to eat anything?" asked Nengi in a concerned tone.

"No! No! I'm okay," replied Bari King as he gently let go of her frame.

Strolling towards a bedside safe, he duly selected its combination and sequestered his pistol inside it. As he began to undress, a sound track, accompanying a Nigerian movie, played in the background. He cast a fleeting glance at the wall and sauntered towards their bathroom. After refreshing himself with cold water and wiping his body dry, he stood before a full length mirror with a gleaming dark skin. His skin-cut hair highlighted facial features that were manly and robust. The refreshing cold bath and the privacy of his luxurious home conspired together and bestowed an overwhelming sense of security and peace on him. Lying down on the bed beside Nengi, he felt insulated from all the cares of the world. Her attention stolen by Bari King, Nengi began to caress his bare chest. Reluctantly and with an apologetic smile, Bari King pulled away from her.

"You know that I'm yet to complete the renewal of the protection ritual, I have been directed to avoid sex for four weeks," stated Bari King in a sedate tone that was meant to soothe Nengi's cloudy countenance.

"I stay at home all day, waiting for you, not knowing wether you'll come home in one piece; do you know how torturous that is? I'm not a piece of decoration in your house; I have feelings you know; right now I feel like holding you, and I care less where ever that leads to. I won't get tired of telling you to abandon your freedom fighter posture and take me away from this village and country; I'm sure you've made quite a tidy sum of money," voiced Nengi in a melancholic tone.

Nengi did not offer any resistance, as he gently pulled her to his chest, with a pacifying expression. Glad about her emotional embrace, Bari King began to stroke the small of her back affectionately. Gently, he laid out Nengi on the bed and appraised her sleeping posture, with a satisfying expression.

Approaching his closed circuit television (CCTV) security system, he ensured that it was functioning properly before he retired to the bed.

Footprints of the morning decorated the atmosphere about them. Bari King and Nengi sat behind a silver dining table with growing appetites fueled by the steaming fresh fish pepper soup and beans pudding. The sound of their voices resonated alone in the whole house and proclaimed Bari King's penchant for privacy. After enjoying their breakfast in peace, Bari King rose up from his chair and ambled towards Nengi. Affectionately holding her two hands, he gently guided her to her feet. Gazing into Bari King's eyes with a look glazed by tender feelings, Nengi stood behind the threshold of the living room vestibule and gently caressed its door knob. Smiling reassuringly at her, Bari King lightly squeezed her left hand and crossed the threshold. Having opened the main entrance door, with an electronic key, he stepped onto the paved walkway. He was dressed in black jeans, matching black sports shoes, and white shirt. His smart and dapper outline bounced confidently on the walkway.

Upon sighting his serious and focused countenance, his men,

seated under the canopy and in the confines of various cars parked within premises, stifled their jokes and banters.

"Let's saddle up and ride," voiced Bari King authoritatively, as he focused his steely attention on his men, who were already scrambling up and hurrying to their vehicles.

Seated in the front of the lead vehicle, Bari King reclined and focused ahead. His mind ruminated over thoughts that underscored his daring nature, while the radio played in the back ground. They drove out of his compound in a convoy of ten vehicles. Their shiny Toyota corolla sedans glistened in the sedate ambiance of the morning; and their guns boosted their confidence and overall sense of invincibility. Bari King sat up as the town hall came into view. Some vehicles were already parked in the outlying grounds. Bari King and his convoy maneuvered into the premises and chose a secluded spot. Bari King, armed with a concealed pistol, advanced towards the entrance of the town hall in the company of ten of his men, who were equally armed with their own pistols. The rest of his men stood guard beside their parked vehicles, with an assortment of heavy caliber automatic and semi-automatic weapons.

Upon sighting Bari King and his men, some men, women, youths and children, who milled about the town hall, hailed Bari King with thunderous shouts of his name. He strode towards his destination with unwavering motions and raised a tightly clenched fist in a reciprocal gesture and acknowledgement. Unpretentious acclaims erupted from the crowd of men, women youths, accommodated inside the town hall, as Bari King stepped inside it. Raising his tightly clenched fist again, he smiled slightly and waved it firmly in acknowledgement. After some fleeting minutes, Bari King gestured with gentle waves of his hand and quieted-down the crowd. The paramount ruler of Kino town, seated on the dais and flanked by the clan Chiefs, managed to mask his irritation and annoyance. He did not participate in the creation of the plaudits bestowed on Bari King and carried on as if nothing of note happened. The paramount ruler, Chief Wikina, as well as the clan Chiefs was bedecked in their traditional, colorful and flowing shirts, hats and walking sticks.

"Shell Petroleum Company has done a lot for our community; they have constructed classroom blocks and health centers for us. This town hall that is sheltering us now was also constructed by them. It is not in our interest to chase them away from our community; we can still benefit more from them," stated Chief Wikina in a pleading tone, as he gazed upon his people.

A hush descended on the crowd, as Bari King advanced towards the podium with a determined expression. Chief Wikina swallowed nervously and shifted his weight on the chair, as Bari King shortened the distance that separated them.

"Do I have your permission to speak?" articulated Bari King calmly, as he gazed at Chief Wikina.

"Yes of course; please go ahead," responded Chief Wikina, without hesitation.

"It is quite understandable for you and your Chiefs, decked up in your flamboyant attire, to sermonize us on how good Shell has been to us; it is no secret that your various country homes were constructed by Shell at no cost to all of you, as a means of ensnaring your respective conscience for their selfish ends. Have you driven around this town of late; a greater section of it is reeking of festering poverty," averred Bari King in a passionate tone.

"But we cannot develop our community alone," interjected Chief Wikina calmly, ignoring his allegations.

The eyes of most of the occupants of the hall beamed with

excitement and expectation. The hush that rested over the crowd wordlessly rooted for Bari King.

"The case you're making for Shell is quite baseless; they have been operating in our community for the past twenty years, and we have nothing to show for it; their attempts at community development are half-hearted and lack serious commitment," continued Bari King with unbridled zest.

"We will not attract anything good by chasing Shell away from our community," replied Wikina as he highlighted his point with vigorous shaking of his head.

"Go and take a look at the so-called health center that they constructed and tell us how many equipment are in them," stated Bari King.

"The ultimatum you gave to Shell will only destroy the peace in this community," said Chief Wikina calmly.

"Are you afraid that the peaceful environment you need to enjoy the illicit money you make from shell, at the detriment of our own people, will cease to exist?" queried Bari King sarcastically.

"Your people are ravaged by poverty and hunger and your popularity is still on a downward spiral," voiced Bari King as he bestowed an unflinching gaze on Chief Wikina, "I propose that we do away with the old patrilineal system of succession to the throne of the paramount ruler and democratically elect a new ruler," continued Bari King in a fervent tone, to deafening shouts of approval from the crowd.

With eyes clad with confusion, Chief Wikina glanced sideways at the seated clan Chiefs; but they failed to provide him with any succor. His brow glistening with sweat; he gazed nervously upon the crowd and swallowed hard. The burgeoning shouts of endorsement to Bari King's proposal, still emanating from the crowd, caused nervous tremors to assail Chief Wikina.

"What you're trying to do is against our customs and traditions; the Government will never recognize any ruler that emerges from this charade," managed Chief Wikina in a steady voice that masked his inner turmoil.

"Customs and traditions are made by the people, and we have united here today as a people to choose another way," declared Bari King confidently.

Under the watchful unsympathetic gaze of his people, Chief Wikina stormed away with some of the clan Chiefs in tow.

"I want to nominate Chief Leba to the vacant throne of traditional ruler; he is a man of conscience and principle; that is why he is always at loggerheads with Chief Wikina; other nominations are welcome," stated Bari King.

"I nominate Chief Asiki," declared an anonymous voice from the crowd.

"I nominate Chief Soko," voiced another anonymous voice.

"It is the wish of the people for all the nominated Chiefs to stand on the podium so as to enable us cue up as our conscience dictates," articulated Bari King, after the nominations ceased.

The three nominated Chiefs obliged and ascended to the podium. Under a free and fair atmosphere, the people broke up into groups and began to cue behind the three Chiefs. Bari King, as the self-appointed election commissioner, counted the various groups of people.

"I hereby declare Chief Leba as the new and elected paramount ruler of Kino town; we can all see that he has a longer line of people," stated Bari King.

The people greeted his announcement with a resounding applause.

"You will write to the state Government and tell them what transpired here today; that we as one have democratically chosen a new paramount ruler for our town," enjoined Bari King firmly, walking up to the chairman and secretary of Kino Development and Survival Union, seated on the podium. Satisfied with their compliant gestures, Bari King turned away from them and proceeded towards the door.

Surrounded by a large group of well wishers, who shook his hand enthusiastically, he smiled as his footsteps became impeded. Sound of extolments offered to him dominated the atmosphere. Finally extricating himself, he walked out of the town hall and headed for his car, with his men close to his heels. He reclined inside his car with a satisfied mien and wondered about Chief Wikina's next move. He counted strongly on his own courage as he explored probable future events. Bari King alighted from his car, as they parked inside his premises, and proceeded towards his main entrance door. Opening the door with his electronic key, he was assailed by agitated voices that continued to rise in crescendo. He quickly closed the door and hurried upstairs, towards the direction of the perceived disturbance, with eyelids stretched by impatience.

2

As Bari King stepped on the first staircase landing, he wringed the features of his face disapprovingly, as he deciphered Nengi's and Oroma's voices from the heated atmosphere that enveloped them.

"Oh not again!" bemoaned Bari King to himself, as he ascended the remaining flight of steps.

"What is going on again?" asked Bari King in a helpless tone, as he opened the door of the family lounge.

"You don't have the right to open my refrigerator and take anything without my permission," declared Nengi in a wrathful tone, as she glared at Oroma.

"Since when did the refrigerator belong to you?" retorted Oroma defiantly.

"Would you ladies please stop!" asserted Bari King in a robust and authoritative voice.

Ireful words, rearing to go, seethed inside Nengi's mind and threatened the peace that reigned about them.

"This thing has to stop," counseled Bari King, in a disapproving tone.

"Tell your sister to respect me as the woman of this house," voiced Nengi calmly, as she turned towards Bari King.

"Respect does not fall `from the sky; you have to earn it," countered Oroma.

"Stop!" barked Bari King.

Gazing at his sister, he smiled faintly and shook his head incredulously.

"Let's go," voiced Bari King calmly, as he looked into Nengi's eyes and wrapped his right arm about her shoulders gently. She did not offer any resistance, as Bari King coaxed her out of the lounge. Her downcast head, resting on Bari King's shoulders, was enfolded by a halo of sadness. Setting her down on the bed with mild motions, he ambled towards his combination safe and secreted his pistol. His medium built frame resting on the bed beside Nengi, he reached out and delicately drew her to his chest.

"Why do you find it difficult to call your sister to order?" queried Nengi despondently.

"We are together now; is it not what matters more than any other thing," replied Bari King calmly.

"But you clearly saw her, as she insulted and disrespected me," continued Nengi.

"I had a long day; let's talk about something more refreshing," cajoled Bari King.

"Don't you care how I feel?" shot Nengi accusingly, as she pulled away from him.

Wearing a blank expression, Bari King rose up from the bed and began to undress. He proceeded into the bathroom and turned on the cold water shower. The sound of the shower drowned the mild sonancy of her sobs.

The morning had few hours to complete the cycle allotted to it by nature.

Bari King leaned against a mango tree inside his compound and gazed skywards. He felt relaxed and contented.

Agitated voices suddenly disrupted the tranquility of his reverie. He moved away from the mango tree and stood firmly on his two feet. Focusing ahead with a heightened sense of alertness, he beheld some of his men as they escorted another man. He noticed that the prodding of his men neutralized the man's reluctance to move forward. When they came within earshot, Bari King discovered that the terror-stricken man was actually one of his own men. His head hung down, the man fidgeted nervously with his fingers.

"We caught him as he attempted to rape a girl," stated Jumbo, Bari King's second in command.

"What!" exclaimed Bari King with an intolerable expression. "Take him far from here and dash one bullet to his right leg. Call the doctor afterward to treat him," commanded Bari King in an unflinching tone.

"Master please forgive me; it was the devil that pushed me into it; I won't do it again," pleaded the man desperately, as sheer terror ravaged the confines of his eyes.

"Take him away form here," snapped Bari King impatiently.

His men surrounded their wayward comrade and sympathetically picked him up.

"Master I won't do it again," entreated the man with renewed urgency as he fell on his knees in a contrite gesture. His despondent entreaties failed to affect the composure of Bari King's receding outline. Once more, they pulled the man to his feet and guided him away. Weakened by despondent feelings, the man's legs caved under him. They propped him on two sides with an undeterred resolve to execute Bari King's sentence.

Noon's exuberance dominated the atmosphere, as Bari King sat under the mango tree. He did not nurture any regret concerning the severe sentence that he passed on his inconstant man.

"Master, I've executed the sentence," reported Jumbo obediently.

"We are going to ride big time on Shell Petroleum. Start putting together a plan for the kidnapping of any of their top official," directed Bari King in a level voice.

"I'll get on with it right away," responded Jumbo

"Look for an inside man that would get us the information we need," counseled Bari King.

"Yes of course master," answered Jumbo.

Bari King nodded his head as a gesture of dismissal and reclined on his chair. Orienting his tall and large frame away from Bari King, Jumbo nurtured several budding thoughts inside his mind.

* * *

Nursing a glass of red wine, Bari King reclined on an easy chair, inside his room, in Presidential Hotel Port Harcourt. He appraised the tidy and pleasant ambience of the room with a satisfied glint in his eyes and smiled at Sonu, his childhood friend.

"Have some more wine and feel good," cajoled Bari King.

"Bari, how can I feel good when I cannot even take care of my family properly?" voiced Sonu as he sighed bitterly.

"But I've been inviting you to ride with us," averred Bari King, with eyes that silently told him about the rich bounties that lay in wait for him.

"I don't think I have the heart to do that," declared Sonu ruefully.

"Well it's your choice, you choose either to remain in your lowly status as a common driver or to become a respected and affluent freedom fighter like me," continued Bari King with a playful smile.

"Most people and newspapers tag you people as criminal militants," stated Sonu in a serious tone.

"Oh! They are just jealous of our boldness and affluence,"

responded Bari King with an unperturbed smile.

"I'm confused here," declared Sonu, as he threw both hands upward in resignation.

"Listen up! I want you to be our inside man in Shell. we are planning a kidnapping operation; you'll be rewarded handsomely afterwards," stated Bari King, sitting up on his chair with a serious expression.

"What! Aaahh! I don't have the liver for that kind of assignment," asserted Sonu with an incredulous expression.

"We are not asking you to take up arms with us and be part of the field operation; we just need some information from you," averred Bari King calmly.

"I'm just a lowly driver in shell; what crucial information can I possibly possess?" uttered Sonu.

"You have plenty to offer; what of your Boss? Is he not a manager," asked Bari King.

"Don't even go there; I don't want to think about what you're suggesting," voiced Sonu vehemently.

"So what are you now? Are you now siding with Shell against your own people; they have drilled crude oil in our town for over twenty years; and what have we to show for it? Sterile farmlands, polluted waters, disease, and poverty stare boldly at us. We must employ every means possible to recover every penny they swindled from us," declared Bari King

"Bari King, your words are too heavy for me," stated Sonu, standing up.

"Sonu, you never disappointed me when we were growing up as kids; I still trust that I'll always count on you," declared Bari King with earnest conviction.

"Bari King, things are different now," responded Sonu as he smiled nostalgically;" Bari, I have to go; my time-off expires by six o'clock," continued Sonu.

"What kind of life are you living? Why are you hurrying home to drive a white man in his car, as if you're a slave on a leash? Come on man! We are no longer in ancient times," expressed Bari King with a visible hint of disapproval lurking in his eyes.

"That's the way it is," voiced Sonu in a tone laced with melancholy.

"It need not be this way; to see you this way rends my heart," expressed Bari King in a dispirited tone of finality.

"Hold on a sec," entreated Bari King, lowering his frame and picking up a bulging big and brown manila envelope, "Take this money; it will see you through some distance; remember there's plenty where that came from," concluded Bari King as he smiled in a conspiratorial manner, with an outstretched arm.

"Bari, why are you tempting me?" asked Sonu calmly, as he fixed an unblinking gaze at the envelope.

"Tempting you? I'm just looking out for you; just like we used to do for each other when we were growing up," responded Bari King in a relaxed tone.

Unenthusiastically, Sonu reached out and collected the money from Bari King.

"Thank you," uttered Sonu in a barely audible voice as he veered away from Bari King and proceeded towards the door.

"You are always welcome in my domain," reassured Bari King, patting him on the back and escorting him to the door.

Standing beyond the threshold of the door, opposite Bari King, Sonu nodded his head gently in a final gesture of appreciation and farewell; Bari King responded with friendly waves of his hand.

Locking the door, he ambled towards the balcony. Assuaged by gusts of fresh air, he stood on the balcony and observed the activity below him. The sight presented by some staff of the traffic enforcement unit of Rivers state Environmental Sanitation Authority, as they struggled with a taxi driver for the keys to his vehicle, highly rankled him. In his mind, he railed against the fact that affluent men with big jeeps and police escorts easily broke traffic offences and got away with it. His attention still focused on Presidential road, he indulged in his favorite pastime of observing and attempting to decipher the expressions on the faces of passersby

Distracted by gentle knocks on the door, he ambled towards it.

"Nengi," voiced Bari King, as he leaned closer to the door.

"Yes! it's me," responded Nengi from the other side.

Upon sighting the two big shopping bags in Nengi's possession, Bari King opened the door very wide for her.

"Your bags are quite full," remarked Bari King, with a patronizing smile, as he sat down.

"Yes the shopping was great; but there's one more skirt I need to have; I don't want to miss it," responded Nengi, as her unabashed smile entreated him.

"You can't be serious," blurted Bari King as he pursed his lips incredulously.

"My purse is depleted; please give me some money; I want to rush back to the shop before they close," continued Nengi in a beseeching tone.

"I can't spare any more money; this is weekend," stated Bari King unwaveringly.

Bari King's firm stance triggered a cloudy reaction on Nengi's face, and she abruptly turned away with disgruntled motions.

* * *

The austere ambience of Sonu's room defied his daydreams and remained unchanged. A pensive expression guarded the features of his face, as images of Bari King flitted to and fro in his mind. Murky emotions sapped his energy as he compared his station as a lowly driver against Bari King's wealthy status. He still dreamed of an affluent life style, though he had no clue how he would make that come true for himself. Glancing at the bulging brown manila envelope, lying beside him on the bed, he shook his head despondently.

"Mr. Sonu!" came a loud imperious voice laced with a thick French ascent and accompanied with haughty knocks on his door.

"Sir!" responded Sonu, jumping to his feet. The familiar voice of his Boss quickened his heartbeat and caused his temples to perspire.

He quickly secreted the brown envelope under his pillow and advanced briskly to the door. Nervously wiping his brow, he opened the door. Mr. Gerard's stern and forbidding countenance instigated a more intense bout of anxiety in his mind.

"Why didn't you make it back by 6 pm," queried Mr. Gerard sternly.

"There was hold-up on the road," responded Sonu meekly.

"You can surely do better than that," retorted Mr. Gerard sarcastically.

"It's true sir," declared Sonu desperately.

"The only truth facing me here is your dumbness; you tell the same lie over and over again; save it for somebody on the same mental level with you," voiced Mr. Gerard.

"I'm sorry sir," blurted Sonu, with a lowered countenance that mimicked a contrite gesture.

"I didn't come here to listen to your litany of woeful words; I came here to give you a last warning," stated Mr. Gerard.

Gazing at Mr. Gerard's retreating outline, Sonu nurtured an

ugly scowl on his face; resentful anger welled up inside him and drowned every other thought. His motions dispirited, Sonu walked back to his room and stretched out on the bed. Mr. Gerard's haughty image flitted to and fro in his mind, and he resented the feelings of smallness that came in its wake and assailed him. He ardently rejected a future borne on the wings of servitude.

The light of the afternoon danced provocatively before Sonu. He stood under a guava tree and waited for his Boss to emerge from the main building. A dark Toyota land cruiser Jeep steamed silently in the background and stole most of his attention away. Spying a faint smudge on the vehicle, he advanced towards it and dabbed at it with a napkin in his possession. Upon sighting Mr. Gerard, he opened a door and sat on the driver's seat. Mr. Gerard's hesitancy beside the vehicle sparked off an unforgiving dread within Sonu's mind. Nursing a frown, Mr. Gerard picked up a nearby twig and gently scratched the underside of the vehicle. The resulting dirty graphics produced by his effort emboldened the frown on his face. Disdainfully, he waved down Sonu. Alighting from the vehicle with a resigned expression, Sonu braced himself.

"Good day sir," greeted Sonu courteously.

"With you, there can be nothing good about any day, because you pollute it with your laziness and dumbness," stated Mr. Gerard, as he pursed his lips contemptuously.

"Sorry sir," blurted Sonu sheepishly.

"What are you sorry about? I guess that sorry is the most popular word in your mind, because of your guilty ways," mocked Mr. Gerard, as he nodded his head knowingly; "why didn't you wash this vehicle properly?" continued Mr. Gerard

"I washed it well sir," responded Sonu, as he creased his face to buttress his stand.

"You washed what well," retorted Mr. Gerard sarcastically; "come over here and see the underside of this vehicle," averred Mr. Gerard, as he authoritatively waved Sonu to his position. His bearing ungraceful, he stood beside Mr. Gerard and avoided his eyes.

"Well don't stand there like a brain-dead zombie; look under the vehicle," berated Mr. Gerard, as he pointed towards the dirty graphics.

Peering sheepishly under the vehicle did not invite any sense of well being into Sonu's mind.

"I'm getting really, really tired of dealing with you; and you know what that means," sounded Mr. Gerard menacingly, as he opened the door of his vehicle.

Dusk played its usual anthem, as Sonu drove into their compound. He was glad that the day's activities were winding down and longed to be free of the oppressive atmosphere created by Mr. Gerard's presence.

"Is that fuel gauge below the half tank," asked Mr. Gerard in an ominous tone.

Briskly glancing apprehensively at the fuel gauge, Sonu felt his entire skin becoming balmy despite the air-conditioned ambience of the vehicle.

"I asked you a question," thundered Mr. Gerard.

"It's below the half tank, sir," replied Sonu apologetically, as he braked in front of the main building.

"I've warned you several times never to allow the fuel gauge to go below the half tank; my words must have been finding it very 'difficult to penetrate your dense consciousness," asserted Mr. Gerard disgustingly.

"Sorry sir," blurted Sonu.

"The discordant sound of your apologies is the last thing I want to hear now," stated Mr. Gerard, with a strong dose of distaste.

"It won't happen again sir," declared Sonu.

"You are the one numbering your days with me," voiced Mr. Gerard menacingly as he opened the door and stepped out of the vehicle.

After parking the vehicle in the garage and handing the keys to the security man, Sonu ambled towards his room with innards bludgeoned by dejected feelings.

* * *

The morning was an impartial witness, as Sonu locked his room. His gait uninspiring, he sauntered towards the Toyota Land Cruiser Jeep. Carefully, he inspected it once more for any visible slur and nodded his head satisfactorily. Sitting behind the steering wheel, he felt the brunt of oppressive feelings.

Not long after Mr. Gerard sat down inside the vehicle, a nasty frown stretched the features of his face.

"Come down! I want to see you properly," Mr. Gerard's tone icy, he alighted from the vehicle.

With rising trepidation, Sonu stepped down from the vehicle. Critically assessing Sonu, Mr. Gerard nurtured a condescending expression.

"Why is your dressing untidy this morning," began Mr. Gerard.

"Untidy?" stammered Sonu.

"Yes untidy! Look at yourself impartially," counseled Mr. Gerard scornfully.

"I don' know how you mean sir," blurted Sonu.

"Your dressing is not passable this morning; untidiness is what I don't want inside my vehicle or around me," he stated with an imperious deportment.

Sonu stole a quick and timorous glance at Mr. Gerard and lowered his head.

"Come on! Take me out of here," commanded Mr. Gerard, as he briskly opened the door of the vehicle and entered it.

* * *

The mellow light of the evening was kind unto the gyrating leaves of trees that towered above Sonu and his companion.

"Who is that man with you? Didn't I warn you not to bring visitors into this compound? Snapped Mr. Gerard as he emerged from the rear of the main building and advanced ominously towards them.

"Sir, he is not really my visitor; he is just a gardener from the opposite compound." Sonu furrowed his forehead in his eagerness to convince Mr. Gerard.

"I refuse to accompany you along your lying path," declared Mr. Gerard sternly.

"Sir, he just came to borrow a file for his cutlass," confessed Sonu, throwing both hands in the air for added emphasis.

"Sir, he is telling the truth," interjected the gardener as he brandished a metal file from an old newspaper and displayed it before Mr. Gerard, "I am already on my way out," concluded the Gardener, as he promenaded briskly towards the main gate.

"You think I am a dullard like you? Do you think that you can confuse me with that little scheme of yours?" stated Mr. Gerard, as his head bobbed to and fro ominously; try this stunt again; and you'll see what I'll do," threatened Mr. Gerard, turning away from Sonu and paying scant attention to the Gardner, who was about to step out of the premises.

Lying down on his bed, Sonu firmly resolved to flee from Mr. Gerard and all he stood for. The desire to avenge all the indignities he suffered in his hands assuaged his despondency. Images of Bari King flashed inside his mind and he reached out for his cell phone.

"Bari, it's me, Sonu!" began Sonu as he spoke into the cell phone in a level tone.

"Sonu my guy! How are you today," responded Bari King amicably from his cell phone.

"Not so good anyway, but I'm feeling much better now," declared Sonu.

"So have you been thinking about the things I said the last time we met?" prodded Bari King gently.

"Yes indeed! And I've just made up my mind to join your movement," declared Sonu firmly.

"Your decision is good," voiced Bari King, in a gladdened tone.

"I've suffered enough at the hands of this French man." Indignation rang out from Sonu's tone.

"We need details of his routine," stated Bari King, in a calm and measured tone.

"I will supply all the information you need; I want the operation to be a very successful one." Sonu's ardent desire for vengeance drowned the gentle voice of his conscience.

"Very good!" averred Bari King.

"We leave the house for work by six-thirty am every morning, and we usually go through Nzimiro street before connecting to Aba Road. He prefers that route. He has just been promoted and will get a mobile police orderly tomorrow," volunteered Sonu.

"Don't worry about the policeman; we'll handle him," declared Bari King confidently.

"Okay." Sonu's tone betrayed his tremendous faith in Bari

King's abilities.

"Sonu, today marks the beginning of better things in your life; the end of your financial challenges are in sight," reassured Bari King.

"I hope so," enthused Sonu.

"I won't give you a particular date; just bear in mind that anything can happen any time." The confidence in Bari King's voice was infectious.

Stretching out once more on the bed, Sonu felt his growing buoyancy.

The inspiring rays of the morning spurred Sonu to long for liberation from his financial difficulties and Mr. Gerard's high-handedness. He wondered if Bari King would strike during the course of the day and set the stage for his dreams to come true. His heart still awash with hopes, he drove out of their compound, situated in the Amadi area of Old GRA, with Mr. Gerard and his mobile police orderly. Seconds after they drove into Nzimiro Street, a black Toyota corolla sedan with tinted glasses maneuvered briskly from the shoulder of the road ahead of them and blocked their front. A second sedan steered towards their rear and hindered it. Nimbly, Bari King alighted from the sedan in front with a drawn pistol and advanced speedily towards the Toyota Land cruiser Jeep.

"Do something!" cried Mr. Gerard as he gazed desperately at the armed mobile policeman.

3

Fearful feelings swamped the mobile policeman and overtook that of Mr. Gerard in intensity. Confused and despairing, the policeman dropped his AK-47 assault rifle on the floor of the vehicle. He shot a quick desperate glance at Mr. Gerard and attempted to forcefully open the door of the vehicle.

"What are you doing," yelled Mr. Gerard.

Bursts of pistol shots from Bari King shattered the windscreen of their vehicle and killed the policeman instantly. Silenced and with mouth wide agape, Mr. Gerard moped at Bari King in disbelief.

"Open the door now," barked Bari King as he banged furiously at Mr. Gerard's side.

Mr. Gerard fidgeted uncontrollably by his side, and as soon as he managed to open the central lock system of the vehicle, Bari King pounced on the door and opened it. Forcefully, he manhandled Mr. Gerard out of the vehicle.

"Move!" snapped Bari King as he herded Mr. Gerard towards the sedan parked ahead of them.

The streets were deserted save for his fiercesome men, armed with AK-47 assault rifles and with shoulders hung with magazines of bullets; they formed a defensive circle around all the vehicles. A distant screeching sound of tyres resonated in the background, as a wary and suspicious commuter bus driver reversed abruptly and fled.

They bundled Mr. Gerard into the sedan and drove away from the scene. They steered into Aba road at an unhurried speed and proceeded towards Eleme junction.

Pressing his back firmly against his seat, Sonu wished for the seat to open up and swallow him up completely. He longed for anything that would save him from the bloody scene presented by his dashboard. He moped ahead with a blank mind, refusing to look at his side, where the slumped and bloody remains of the policeman lay, or at himself, stained by the policeman's blood. He managed to steady himself and remain calm during the course of the whole melee as directed by Bari King. Teams of policemen arrived forty-five minutes after the incident and still encountered his static and mopey countenance.

Unchallenged, Bari King and his men drove through the long stretch of Aba road with their captive and ended up in Kino town. They drove towards the banks of Kino River and steered Mr. Gerard into a waiting white launch with outboard engines.

"Where are you taking me to?" blurted Mr. Gerard in a frightened voice.

"Shut up," barked Bari King.

They sped away on the calm waters and headed towards the thick rain forest that bordered their town. They anchored the boat close to the edge of the rainforest and directed Mr. Gerard, who moped like someone with compromised mentation, out of boat.

With Mr. Gerard sandwiched in between them, they advanced into the forest along a foot-path. The chatter of monkeys resonated from the towering trees and competed with that of birds for dominance.

The massive coils of a large python, squeezing life out of a juvenile antelope, suddenly loomed before them and they halted in their tracks.

"Take your right," commanded Bari King calmly.

They detoured round the python and its prey and continued onwards. With a trembling hand, Mr. Gerard wiped perspiration from his brow.

"Elephants ahead," cautioned the lead man.

"Take another right," directed Bari King.

The trumpeting sound emitted by a troop of elephants became clearer and louder, as they side-stepped them.

"What is this place?" blurted Mr. Gerard, daring not to look back. He failed to discover any means of conquering his despair.

"You are now in the jungle, Frenchman, and you better behave," uttered Bari King sternly.

The artificial sonance of motorbikes suddenly pierced the atmosphere and disrupted the natural rhythmic sounds of the forest.

"They're here," voiced the lead man

Five motorbikes in a single row, manned by well armed men, appeared before them.

"Boss!" chorused the bikers as they alighted form their bikes and bowed respectfully towards Bari King's direction.

Bari King responded by vigorously swaying a tightly clenched fist in mid-air. Briskly, the men reversed their bikes and their comrades distributed themselves among them. From his position at the back of a bike, Bari King sternly motioned at Mr. Gerard with his head, and he quickly transformed his unsure gestures and clambered onto the back of a waiting bike. They drove for some minutes along a cleared path in the forest and ended up in a circular clearing.

With renewed trepidation, Mr. Gerard gazed at the numerous military-style tents, satellite dish and communication mast, all coated with green camouflage paint. Behind protective sandbags, Bari King's men manned machine gun positions, strategically located around the clearing.

"Take him to the guest tent on the right," directed Bari King as he glanced authoritatively at his men and disembarked from the motorbike. Amidst reverential gestures directed at him by his men, he went straight to his own tent, distinguished from the rest by its sheer size.

"Move!" barked Jumbo

A mixture of fear and confusion rendered Mr. Gerard immobile.

"I said move!" snarled Jumbo, ominously drawing closer to Mr. Gerard.

Recovering a measure of his composure, he began to move towards the direction indicated by Jumbo with unmetrical footsteps. Jumbo overtook him and halted beside a neat tent. Responding to his hand gestures, Mr. Gerard entered the tent without further hesitation. Hopelessness kept a firm grip on his innards as he glanced at the small mattress and pillow, standing bedside lamp that illuminated the tent, and standing fan. His whole body awash with tepid perspiration, he collapsed on top of the pillow case and bed sheet that lay on the mattress.

Startled by Bari King's sudden and unannounced entrance, Mr. Gerard sat up abruptly on the mattress.

"If you want to answer the call of nature, my men will take you to the pit toilet situated at the back of the clearing," began Bari King in an unmoving voice.

"Pit toilet!" blurted Mr. Gerard in a frightened voice.

"Yes, pit toilet," responded Bari King calmly. "We have a water closet system here, but I want you to have a little taste of the poverty that ravages my people; poverty that your company turns a blind eye on," declared Bari King.

"We have not done anything wrong to your people," stammered Mr. Gerard.

"Your company has been taking oil from our land for over twenty years, and where has that left us?" queried Bari King, his eyes unfazed.

"You should pose that question to your Chiefs and elites," averred Mr. Gerard Pleadingly.

"It is not enough to lay all the blame at the footsteps of our Chiefs and so called elites; if your company was really interested in bettering the lot of the common people, they should have adopted a more balanced and creative approach that would permit whatever goodies they have to offer to trickle down to the grassroots," expressed Bari King.

"What has that got to do with me? I'm not my company," said Mr. Gerard in a plaintive voice.

"Are you trying to disown your company? I hate traitors whether they are on my side or not!" The hard edge in Bari King's tone frightened the living the daylights out of Mr. Gerard's face.

His heart pounding furiously, Mr. Gerard was at loss on how he would navigate through the tense moments. Lowering his countenance was the only defense mechanism left to him. Unmindful of his fearful state, Bari King stormed out of his tent.

Mr. Gerard collapsed on the bed and gazed upwards with a blank expression

"Come out! Lunch is about to be served," bellowed Jumbo close to the entrance of Mr. Gerard's tent.

"Follow me!" commanded Jumbo, as he led the way. Mr. Gerard wondered about the nature of the lunch that lay in wait for him, with a mixture of curiosity and foreboding.

They entered a large area, constructed of sandcrete blocks and corrugated aluminum sheets, that functioned as the kitchen and serving area. Out of steaming pots, supported on industrial gas cookers, some men served other men that cued in a single file.

Upon sighting Mr. Gerard, Bari King left the middle of the line and ambled towards him.

"Frenchman! There will be no special treatment for you; you'll eat what we eat and wash your plates afterwards, just like every other person; lunch is pounded yam with native soup, and I hope you'll like it," voiced Bari King with a mischievous grin.

"Native soup?" blurted Mr. Gerard with controlled alarm.

"It is prepared with fish, shrimp and other sea foods, if that will be a source of consolation to you." Bari King was clearly enjoying himself.

"Why are you punishing me?" Deep tones of lamentation characterized Mr. Gerard's voice as he shook his head despondently.

"For now you are the face of your company, and you better watch it." The ominous transformation on Bari King' face caused Mr. Gerard to stiffen up. With great unease, he looked away from him. "Go to the back and join the cue if you wish; the choice is yours if you want to starve," concluded Bari King as he ambled back to the middle of the line.

His motions poor in enthusiasm, Mr. Gerard sauntered to the back of the line and cued up.

With his own tray of food, Bari King strolled back to his tent without batting an eyelid towards Mr. Gerard's direction.

Harboring great uncertainty, Mr. Gerard lifted a silver tray from a stack and adorned it with breakable flat and soup plates. Doubtfully, he picked up a wrap of pounded yam and drifted towards the array of silverwares that bore the soup, fish and other assorted sea foods. He hesitated before the container of soup and moped at the steward, who motioned with his hand for him to serve himself. As he dished out the soup into his own plate, a mixture of muffled and full blown laughter, from Bari King's men, rang out in the arena. Ignoring their boisterousness, Mr. Gerard trudged back to his tent with his tray of food. He sat the tray on the linoleum floor and regarded the food with a mixture of hopelessness and incredulity. He was undecided about his approach, but he finally decided to chew on the pounded yam instead of swallowing it. As he spooned the pounded yam and soup into his mouth, he allowed a gesture of acceptance to become visible on his face. His drive to survive spurred him to wolf down the remaining pounded yam and soup. Shortly after ingesting the food, he experienced a discomforting rumble in his stomach. Clutching at the two sides of his stomach with a contorted expression, he rushed out of his tent.

Leaning on a nearby tree, Bari King appraised him with an indifferent expression.

"I need to go," blurted Mr. Gerard in an urgent voice, as he gaped at Bari King.

"Take him to the pit toilet," commanded Bari King, with a steely focus that intimidated Mr. Gerard.

"Please allow me to use your water closet," entreated Mr. Gerard.

"It's either the pit toilet or your trousers; choose one," responded Bari King with unpretentious apathy.

Orienting himself towards the progressing footsteps of one of Bari King's men, he trailed after him. Unmindful of the mixture of dread and discomfitures betrayed by the expression on Mr. Gerard's face, the man pointed at an outbuilding situated very close to the perimeter of the clearing and retraced his steps. Standing before the door of the toilet, he glanced sideways in a bid to delay the inevitable moments he would spend inside it. His stomach rumbled mercilessly and sent him scurrying into the toilet. With mitigated dread, he realized that the insides of the toilet were clean. Emerging from the toilet after relieving himself, he ambled towards a nearby standing tap and washed his hands.

"I can see you're adapting very well," voiced Bari King with a mischievous grin as Mr. Gerard passed him. Regarding him briefly with a blank expression, Mr. Gerard focused his attention back in the direction of his tent.

Mr. Gerard stretched himself on the bed inside his tent and sought once more to educate his mind to accept his present situation and hope for the best.

"Open this tent," barked Bari King as he stood in front of Mr. Gerard's tent.

The forbidden tone in Bari King's voice sent Mr. Gerard scurrying towards the entrance of the tent. Nervously unzipping the tent, he wondered if his luck would take a turn for the worse.

"Tomorrow we make our phone calls," stated Bari King severely as he peered into the tent. Evading his eyes, Mr. Garrard looked downwards.

The sight of Bari King's retreating outline failed to ameliorate his dread.

Cueing up in line for dinner, Mr. Gerard ignored the amusing gestures and glances directed at him by Bari King's men. The clearing was brightly lit-up and security lighting illuminated the far reaches of the forest.

Through side netting that facilitated ventilation inside the tent, he appraised the bustling camp and wondered how he would fare through the rest of the night.

He suddenly woke up with a start. Beads of perspiration claimed his face, and an oppressive tiredness made his innards raw. His inability to put off the lone bulb that illuminated the tent compounded his frustration and sorrow. Sluggishly raising his left arm, he realized that the time was just fourteen minutes after one. With shoulders hung with gloom, he sat up on the foam.

With a groggy head and a somewhat disoriented sense, he greeted the light of the morning. Standing up listlessly, he stretched himself in a bid to invoke some vitality into his entire being.

"Open this tent," commanded Bari King, as he stood before it.

Rush of panic quelled some of his lethargy, and he hurried towards the entrance of the tent.

"You'll go down to the stream and take your bath with the boys," began Bari King.

"Surely you must have some passable bathroom here," blurted Mr. Gerard as he struggled to control his exasperation

"It's your choice to bath or not to bath," voiced Bari King apathetically.

"But I've never done that before," divulged Mr. Gerard.

"There's always a first time; imagine it to be a recreational swim." His mischievous grin was unsympathetic to Mr. Gerard.

"I don't know how to swim," disclosed Mr. Gerard helplessly.

"They will point you to the shallow end of the stream," stated Bari King," I'll be back in forty-five minutes time for the phone calls; get the numbers ready," concluded Bari King. His face broke out into a mischievous grin once more, as he turned away from Mr. Gerard.

Taking a few tentative steps away from Mr. Gerard, Bari King swerved his head backwards and pursed his lips in a sportive gesture. Mr. Gerard, transfixed by helplessness, paid little heed to him.

Scores of men, with shoulders hung with different types of towels, trooped past Mr. Gerard. He suspected that they were heading towards the stream to have their morning bath. He managed to heal his thoughts of their vacillation and sauntered into his tent. Picking up a neatly folded towel that lay by the side of the bed, he ambled out of the tent and joined a band of men. To ignore the amusing glances exchanged by the men, he maintained a straight face. They walked a short distance from the clearing and stopped at the banks of a clear and gentle-flowing stream. The stream was bounded by tall trees with massive branches, colonized by lively birds that chirped away cheerfully. Robust banters exchanged by the men dominated the air waves.

"Please where is the shallow end?" asked Mr. Gerard, with an air of resignation as he gazed into the face of a nearby man.

"Continue walking down; I'll tell you when to stop," replied the man.

Obeying the man, he began to walk along the banks of the stream.

"You can stop now," directed the man, "the portion of the stream facing you is not deep; you can wade in," concluded the man.

With insecure motions, he removed his trouser and shirt. Ignoring the boisterous cackles of the men that flew across his face, Mr. Gerard cagily ambled towards the stream and carefully dipped an exploratory right leg into the waters.

"Go on the water is not deep there," encouraged the man.

As he relaxed his guard and stretched his right leg further, he fell into the water. The water swallowed his entire frame. As he managed to surface, sheer terror oozed from his eyes. He opened his mouth to shout, but it filled with water very quickly, and he only managed to emit a gurgling sound. Desperate falling of his hands against the water only elicited roaring laughter from the men about him. As he went down again, he felt a firm arm about his wrist, and the tormenting panic that caused his entire frame to vibrate receded away. Awash with relief, he surfaced again, under the guidance of one of the men.

"Please take me ashore," blurted Mr. Gerard breathlessly.

His rescuer gently dragged him ashore and bestowed a bemused grin on him. Breathing heavily, he tugged himself to the trunk of a fallen tree and leaned against it. Beholding large numbers of the men as they clambered ashore, he reached out for the towel and his clothes. Tiredly, he stood up and dried his body. As they marched through the forest, he paid little heed to the unending banters exchanged by the men.

He collapsed on the bed inside his tent and shook his head despondently.

"Open this tent now," barked Bari King, as he stood in front of it.

Startled, Mr. Gerard rose up abruptly and hurried towards the entrance of the tent.

"How did you enjoy your swim," asked Bari King, sporting an impish smile.

For some fleeting seconds and with a blank expression, Mr. Gerard gazed at him. He stepped out of the way, as Bari King sauntered across the threshold of the tent.

"Take your phones and get the number of your Boss," continued Bari King, as he handed two mobile phones to Mr. Gerard.

Accepting the phones with a heavy sense of foreboding, Mr. Gerard turned them on and began to search through their contents.

"Here is the number," stated Mr. Garrard in a burdensome tone, as he meekly conveyed one of his phones to Bari King. Afloat with feelings of invincibility, Bari King brandished his Thuraiya satellite phone from his jeans pocket. He dialed the number highlighted on Mr. Gerard's phone and then waited.

"This is Bari King of Niger Delta Protection Force; we have your man, Mr. Gerard. If you want to see him alive again, you must arrange gold bullion bars worth one billion naira in the international market; hold on first for your man," voiced Bari King in an icy and ominous tone.

"Henri! Are you okay?" came the voice from the other end of the phone.

"I'm okay for now but time may be running out for me," replied Mr. Gerard in a woebegone tone.

"Are they treating you well?" asked his Boss in a clear tone of urgency.

"I'm being held in some kind of ..." continued Mr. Gerard, as the phone was forcefully snatched away from him before he could complete his statement.

"Henri are you okay?" blurted his Boss.

"You heard his voice; and I assume that you heard mine even clearer," asserted Bari King.

"What you're demanding is too much?" articulated Mr. Gerard's Boss in a stressed voice.

"That's just a fraction of what your company has stolen from us," voiced Bari King defiantly.

"Gold bullion bars? Where did that come from?" queried Mr. Gerard's Boss pensively.

"I get you now! You believe that we are all ill-exposed and backward villagers; don't allow your surprise to overwhelm you." expressed Bari King, grinning triumphantly, "Now listen carefully, I'll call you again in three days time to tell you the time limit and drop zone; if you try to toy around with me, the drop zone will become the kill zone for your colleague," threatened Bari King ominously, as he cut off the line abruptly.

He fixed a portentous glance at Mr. Gerard, who gently shifted his eyes away from him.

"Your people had better behave or something bad will happen to you." His face still flaunted an unrelenting sinister expression. "There's somebody dying to meet you," continued Bari King. "Sonu come on in," he beckoned, mischievously grinning at Mr. Gerard.

Beholding Sonu as he sauntered into the tent with a defiant swagger, Mr. Gerard's jaw dropped in shock.

"Sonu! So you're involved," blurted Mr. Gerard with eyes and demeanor taunted by disbelief.

"So what are you going to do about it?" challenged Sonu boldly.

"What am I going to do about it? You won't get away with it," stated Mr. Gerard with features flushed with anger.

"Shut up!" barked Bari King menacingly," If I hear any more word from you again, I will invoke something very terrible upon you'" continued Bari King.

Recoiling away from Bari King, Mr. Gerard surrendered the expression on his face unto fear. Sonu grinned with satisfaction at the sight of his subdued former Boss.

"So who's the Boss now?" taunted Sonu, as he flaunted scornful gestures of his head before him.

With expressionless eyes, Mr. Gerard threw a second's glance at Sonu and turned away.

"Sonu you're this! You're that! Your brain needs to be examined! You're a dunce, you're a retard, etc." recited Sonu with a nasty expression. "So what are you now? The almighty Mr. Gerard? No! There's no difference between you and a frightened little mouse," continued Sonu venomously.

Bari King chuckled and patted Sonu gently on the back.

"Relax man, the past is behind you now; we are looking forward to bigger and better things," expressed Bari King, as he smiled reassuringly at Sonu.

"If your people don't co-operate, this African soil will swallow you up, and the sacrifice won't be enough to compensate for all that your people ripped off from our land," declared Bari King ominously.

Turning away from Mr. Gerard, he signaled to Sonu, and they promenaded out of the tent.

Sitting up on an easy chair inside his spacious tent, Bari King turned his satellite receiver and engaged CNN network. He reclined back on the chair and focused his attention on the television.

"Boss! It's me, Jumbo," voiced Jumbo outside Bari King's tent.

"Come on in," beckoned Bari King as he sat up.

"There's a CNN reporter nosing around, in the village, and asking about you," reported Jumbo, as he stood before Bari King.

"I see," responded Bari King pensively.

"Boss what do you advice?" continued Jumbo.

"Arrange and take him to Camp Two, tomorrow morning; we'll meet there," directed Bari King, after some seconds thought.

"Yes Boss," voiced Jumbo, as he turned and marched out of the tent.

With a preoccupied mind, Bari King reclined on his chair. Mentally, he began to explore various paths that would maximize his gains from the proposed encounter with the CNN reporter.

The morning, still bright and cheerful, witnessed lilting chirping of birds, as it inspired the gyrating leaves of trees.

Bari King and five of his men, heavily armed with AK-47 assault rifles, boarded a well conditioned launch, equipped with a machine gun. The ripples created by the fast launch disturbed the calmness that reigned over the waters. For miles, they encountered no boat. Then the whirring sound of another invisible launch that approached them from the distance stirred them to attention and heightened their alertness. They relaxed when they realized that the approaching lunch, completing another round of patrol, was one of their own.

"Master!" chorused the heavily armed men, vigorously swaying tightly clenched fists in mid-air, as they passed them.

Meandering through the waters for about forty-five minutes, they anchored the boat close to a shore and disembarked.

"Master!" hailed an assembly of men on the banks of the river. Their heavy arms and ammunition heightened their fearsome looks.

Nodding his head in response, Bari King gestured impatiently with his hands. All his thoughts were focused towards their destination. Leaving three men behind, to guard their launch, they began to pound on a well-worn footpath with some liveliness. After twelve minutes, they arrived at another camp similar to the one they left behind, with machine gun nests guarding its perimeter.

Welcomed by robust cheers and greetings from his men, Bari King marched into the camp. Upon sighting the CNN reporter and his crew, he ambled towards them with a relaxed expression.

"You're welcome to our camp," began Bari King, as he smiled courteously and extended his right hand towards the reporter. The reporter rose up and politely shook Bari King. He shook hands with the two members of the reporter's crew and sat down opposite the reporter.

"I'm Jeff Konig from CNN, and I'm here with my crew," began the reporter in a business -like manner.

"I'm Bari King, and what exactly do you want to hear from me; I understand that you're very keen to talk to me," voiced Bari King calmly.

Jeff Konig signaled to his crew; and they setup their camera and other ancillary equipment.

"The world would like to know where you're coming from; and the motives that drive your movement," asked the reporter.

"Where I'm coming from?" stated Bari King with an amusing chuckle; "well I'm coming from a place ravaged by oil pollution; from a people that are plagued by poverty, because their resources are being taken away from them without adequate compensation," averred Bari King passionately.

"Shell Petroleum Development Company claims to have spent a lot of money on community development," continued Jeff Konig.

"I understand you explored many nooks and crannies of my village; so what did you see? Can you deny the grinding poverty that is eating away at the souls of my people? Did you see much evidence of community development?" voiced Bari King in a sober tone.

"What about your leaders? Perhaps they have some answering to do," pressed Jeff Konig.

"It's always expedient for Shell to pass the blame unto the community leaders; but let me tell you one thing; it is the explicit plan of Shell to empower a few people in the community, whom they believe could box the people into a corner and scorch any seed of agitation in their minds; that tactic is old fashioned now; it won't work anymore," declared Bari King.

"What do you consider yourself to be?" Jeff Konig looked keenly at him.

"I'm a freedom fighter; and I'm striving to liberate my people from the shackles of poverty and environmental degradation, with the resources we have here." Bari King's stance was unmoving.

"You banished Shell from your community; how has that affected your people," asked Jeff Konig.

"The ousting of Shell is only affecting a corrupt few, who masquerade as community leaders," voiced Bari King contemptuously.

"So the generality of the people are not missing them?" queried Jeff Konig.

"Shell has been operating in our community for over twenty years; and in all that period, they have been flaring gas and rendering our farmlands sterile; the environmental pollution that trails their activities brings respiratory and skin diseases to my people; not to talk of the damaging black acid rain; tell me why we should miss them," asserted Bari King. His passion and seriousness intermingled and erased every doubt in his mind.

"Shell claims that some of the environmental pollution in your community is caused by deliberate acts of vandalization from your people, in order to claim some form of compensation from the situation," posed Jeff Konig.

"Shell is fond of presenting lame excuses; they might as well claim that my people are responsible for flaring gas here; are you aware that the United Nations Environment Program recently indicted Shell for their activities in my area?" stated Bari King in a convincing tone.

"I spoke to a lot of people in the village, and you're quite some benefactor to them," expressed Jeff Konig,"

"I try for my people," replied Bari King without any airs.

"You must be spending quite some fortune to maintain your camp and sustain your operations; how do you manage," queried Jeff Konig.

"We survive from our land," stated Bari King.

"When you say 'we survive from our land' does it mean that

you have appropriated the resources that abound in your locality including crude oil," asked Jeff Konig.

"Well I'm not at liberty to elaborate on that; let's just leave at that." A coy smile creased the features of Bari King's face.

"In the ultimatum you gave to Shell, you demanded for half of the open market value of crude oil drilled in your locality on behalf of your community. Shell is not empowered by your Federal government to effect such payments. Does it mean that Shell or any other oil company is not welcome in your community?" asked Jeff Konig.

"The Federal Government has terribly let us down; they take our resources and abandon us to ruin, poverty and utter degradation. Enough! We have taken matters into our own hands. We are holding Shell accountable, because they are the ones here, drilling our oil," asserted Bari King.

"There are reports of rape and brazen brutalization committed against some members of communities within this locality. What is your position on that?" asked Jeff Konig.

"What did you hear about me in the village?" asked Bari King calmly.

"They spoke highly of you in most quarters," replied Jeff Konig.

"Do you think that I'm the kind of person that would tolerate shitty behaviour. The litany of shit you recited does not happen in the areas under my control and protection. Yes I admit that we have bad eggs masquerading as freedom fighters, but their days are numbered." His stern voice did not come with any apologies.

"So do you have any kind of structure within the militant ranks for sanitizing and keeping the members of the various militant groups in line," queried Jeff Konig.

"That is none of your business," asserted Bari King.

"The spates of kidnappings within Port Harcourt and environs have created a strong climate of insecurity within the town, and this has led to mass exodus of expatriates and top management staff of Nigerian descent, working in oil companies and other institutions. Unemployment has increased; you have a lot of cooks and drivers who are now redundant," opined Jeff Konig.

"A lot of the kidnappings are criminally motivated, and if we catch such criminals, regretting the day they were born will be an understatement," averred Bari King.

"Are you saying that kidnapping could be justified on certain grounds even when its effects are adverse on your own people?" Jeff Konig's pinpoint concentration remained unwavering.

"We are freedom fighters; and we will employ all available means to right the wrongs that have been perpetuated against my people for so long. No company or Government will hide behind the scenes anymore and rob us of what rightfully belongs to us; our crude oil should uplift us not impoverish us. We are fighting for a better tomorrow, and any of our brothers who are suffering now should employ more patience and bear with us," articulated Bari King.

"Your movement recently kidnapped a top executive of Shell petroleum; what will become of him if his company fails to pay the ransom of one billion naira worth of gold bullion bars? inquired Jeff Konig.

"Let's wait and see," stated Bari King.

"The Nigerian police has proved ineffective against your movement and other militant groups in the Niger Delta; it's just a matter of time before the military joins the fray; won't that spell the end of your resistance?" speculated Jeff Konig

"The Nigerian police is motivated by greed, while I and my men are motivated by a noble cause," declared Bari King.

"But the military is different," volunteered Jeff Konig.

"Can you bet your life on that? Anyway we are ready for any opposing force that would chance our way," stated Bari King confidently, standing up and signaling the end of the interview session.

"Thank you very much for your time Sir," said Jeff Konig politely.

"I wish you the best," replied Bari King.

Turning towards Jumbo, Bari King directed him to a spot, away from Jeff Konig and his crew.

"See that they get a safe passage out of this place," ordered Bari King, as Jumbo came within ear-shot.

"Yes Boss ," accented Jumbo.

Briskly, Bari King strode towards the banks of the river. An armed retinue of his men formed a protective band behind him, as his confidence grew in stature. They boarded their launch and sped off.

Arriving back at their camp, Bari King retired straight to his tent.

Leaning against a tree, Sonu nurtured a mocking smile on his face a he gazed at Mr. Gerard. The sight of Mr. Gerard washing his clothes beside his tent fed his vengeful spirit. As Sonu's smile transformed into a full blown laugher, Mr. Gerard's attention was piqued and he turned towards Sonu.

"Mr. high-and-mighty is now washing his own clothes," began Sonu in a mocking tone.

"Mr. Gerard restrained himself from uttering any word as his own mouth opened.

"You can't find your tongue any more? How is that?" continued Sonu.

Mr. Gerard ignored him and continued washing his clothes.

"You think that you can come all the way from France and lord over us here; look at you now," voiced Sonu in a sinister tone as he walked away.

Bari King reclined on an easy chair inside his tent and flipped through a news paper. He craved for peaceful feelings, as he attempted to quieten the numerous thoughts that populated his mind.

"Boss! Boss!" shouted Jumbo in an urgent tone outside Bari King's tent.

Jumping to his feet, Bari King's retrieved his pistol and rushed out of the tent.

4

Barefooted and brimming with alertness, Bari King stood before Jumbo.

"What is it?" queried Bari King impatiently.

"Alali was attacked in Port Harcourt today; he is in a critical condition," blurted Jumbo breathlessly.

"Attacked?" uttered Bari King incredulously.

"Who can that be? Who is playing in the lion's den?" ejaculated Bari King as he ruminated aloud to himself, nodding his head haughtily.

"Boss! from the information filtering to me, I believe the attack was ordered by Power Donga," related Jumbo.

"Power Donga? Where did he get the backbone to stand and raise a finger against one of my men," stated Bari King, with furrowed temples.

"Boss he is definitely the one," restated Jumbo.

"Okay! Okay!" blurted Bari King, with a faraway look in his eyes, as he went back to his tent.

With a renewed sense of urgency, he rushed out of the tent again.

"Keep the men in a state of heightened alert," ordered Bari King, hurrying back to his tent.

"Yes Boss," responded Jumbo.

Pacing to and fro in his tent, he permitted countless thoughts to runn riot in his mind. Restraining the urge to hurriedly lead his men into Power Donga's camp became an uphill task for him. He finally sat down on the chair and reached out for his satellite phone.

"Hello Major; I have a situation on my hands now; Power Donga attacked one of my men; I'm battling hard to restrain myself from riding right now to his camp to finish him and his men," ejaculated Bari King.

"Take a breather man! Relax and maintain tactical discipline; you're wise in not rushing off to Power Donga's camp; has it occurred to you that this could be a trap?" came the voice of the major, a retired military officer and Bari King's military adviser, from the other end of the line.

"Yes it has crossed my mind; but I trust my steely constitution to run over any obstacle that he will spring my way," vaunted Bari King in a robust tone.

"Take it easy; you know your camps are situated at very strategic and lucrative sites; you are bound to become a target, if you become hasty; don't forget that," continued the major.

"Any body that targets me is only daring the wrath of a merciless lion," declared Bari King.

"Let's get down to specifics now; we need to strategize with adequate inputs of deception, concealment and surprise," suggested the major.

"What do you have in mind?" asked Bari King, somewhat calmer.

"You are much more buoyant than Power Donga, that's an advantage; we'll try and infiltrate his camp with some juicy offers of financial inducements. I'm sure some of his men will fall; he doesn't take good care of his men; he is known to be greedy." The major's conspiratorial tone sounded quite convincing to Bari King.

"That's sounds good; I'll tell Jumbo to start fleshing out a plan; he's good with things like that," stated Bari King in a buoyant tone.

"You can also put a deceptive plan in place: make reconciliatory overtures of peace to him and lull him into a false sense of security," added the major.

"Yeah that's good," declared Bari King, sounding elated, "major thank you very much; we'll definitely talk again," concluded Bari King.

"Any time man!" responded the major.

Reclining on his chair, Bari King reached out for his shortwave radio.

"Jumbo, see me in my tent now," directed Bari King as he spoke into the radio.

"Yes Boss," responded Jumbo from his own handset.

Setting the portable handset down, Bari King restlessly paced to and fro in his tent. Myriad of thoughts, yearning to be transformed into tangible plans, roamed freely in his mind.

"Boss I'm here," came Jumbo's voice outside Bari King's tent.

"Come in right away," replied Bari King, impatiently.

Jumbo stood before Bari King with a receptive attention and eager consciousness.

"We are going to ride big time on Power Donga, but we're going to be very methodical in delivering a crushing blow on him and his men. We are going to infiltrate his camp; you will fashion out a plan for reaching out to some of his men with juicy financial inducements; I want it to be fast, sharp, and furious," directed Bari King with keen concentration.

"I'll get on with it right away Boss," replied Jumbo, with enthusiastic airs.

Cheerful chirping of birds and flourishing calls of monkeys

pointed Bari King's awareness towards the delicate light of the morning. Standing in front of his tent, he smiled at playful antics of agile monkeys, gamboling atop tall trees. The rich and seducing greenness of the foliage inspired soothing feelings inside him. Soaking in the natural and calming sights of the morning, presented by the forest, became the preoccupation of his consciousness. Reluctantly, he turned away and focused his attention on his tent. Picking up his portable and powerful transistor radio, he sat down on a chair. He tuned the frequency to the local radio station. Paying little attention to the audio, streaming from the radio, he relaxed his body on the chair. His consciousness suddenly prodded by a familiar voice, Bari King sat bolt upright on the chair and listened intently to the radio.

"Honorable Kibara!" exclaimed Bari King, nodding his head furiously.

"The Niger Delta Protection Force is a terrorist organization; it does not enjoy my support, and I'm certainly sure that the generality of Niger Deltans disapprove of it. Kidnapping is a heinous crime; I don't have any kind word for them or their leader. All their pursuits are selfishly and criminally motivated; they don't have the interest of Niger Delta at heart. All the illicit money they generate from kidnapping and illegal crude oil bunkering are funneled to service selfish wants and desires. Militancy in the Niger-Delta is a threat to peaceful co-existence, life and livelihood. The Niger-Delta protection force should realize that they are desecrating our land with their infamous activities, and their status is no different from outcasts of old," came the sure voice of Honorable Kibara, the speaker on the radio.

"Outcasts!" ejaculated Bari King, seething with anger.

Standing up abruptly from the chair, he flaunted a far-way expression that thinly veiled very ominous threats directed at

Honorable Kibara.

"We'll see," ruminated Bari King aloud to himself.

The rest of the interview drifted from the radio and formed an unwanted background to Bari King's dastardly plans against Honorable Kibara.

Sitting down on the chair, he picked up his shortwave radio handset.

"Jumbo, let me have the latest surveillance report on Honorable Kibara," voiced Bari King through the handset.

"'Right away Boss; just give me a few seconds," responded Jumbo from his own set.

The venom in Bari King's thought against Honorable Kibara continued to rise with the moments.

"Boss I'm here," stated Jumbo in front of Bari King's tent.

"Come right in," beckoned Bari King with keenness.

Jumbo marched in and handed him a brown manila envelop. Impatiently, Bari King opened it and retrieved a neatly bound profile. He thumbed through its non-voluminous pages and set it down on his laps.

"So he's still whoring about town," blurted Bari King, as he glanced at Jumbo.

"Yes Boss he still plays around with his mistress," responded Jumbo, smiling mischievously.

"And he is stupid enough to use the same guesthouse over and over again," voiced Bari King distastefully.

"Yes Boss- the same one at GRA Phase II; he's often there most weekends with his mistress; she settles in before him," disclosed Jumbo.

"I gather there are two luxurious suites in the guesthouse, and he uses either of them; get our men to pay for the two suites before the weekend and plant hidden cameras about the beds. I want all the details of his extramarital escapades to be captured electronically," directed Bari King.

"No problem Boss!" accented Jumbo.

"How far have you gone with the Power Donga operation? Querried Bari king.

"We're on course Boss; additional plans are on the way to sabotage their gunboats," related Jumbo.

"Good! Good!" enthused Bari King; "get on with the other operation immediately," concluded Bari King.

"Right away Boss," responded Jumbo, as he briskly detoured away from Bari King.

Cries of insects and other nocturnal animals celebrated the enveloping darkness in the forest. Bari King and a large retinue of his men, well- armed with a variety of automatic and semiautomatic weapons, stood on the banks of the river. Waves of relief coursed through his veins as the headlamps of an approaching boat illuminated their surroundings.

Mr. Wong, his Chinese business partner, emerged from the boat and stepped onto the banks of the river. Bari King ambled towards him and warmly shook hands with him.

"Welcome back my friend," hailed Bari King.

"Thank you very much; it's good to see you in good health," responded Mr. Wong with a strong American accent.

"I'm good always; I'm here; I'm not going anywhere," vaunted Bari King.

"That means many years of fruitful relationship between us," expressed Mr. Wong with a big smile.

"Sure man!" exclaimed Bari King.

"I brought very tidy and serious weapons and equipment; I'm certain you'll like them," enthused Mr. Wong, as he sauntered towards the boat, "let's go and have a look," continued Mr. Wong.

"I'm right behind you," stated Bari King, walking behind Mr. Wong with eager footsteps.

They boarded the large boat and advanced to its rear compartment. A large assortment of weapons flaunted their shiny surfaces before them.

"I brought the night vision goggles, grenade launchers, automatic and semiautomatic assault rifles, pistols, and plentiful ammunition," raved Mr. Wong, "try the night vision goggles now; you'll love them," continued Mr. Wong, opening a green metal container and retrieving a black leather case. Unzipping the leather bag, he handed a specimen goggle to Bari King.

"This is amazing!" declared Bari King, as he fitted the goggles to his face and peered into the darkness.

With Bari King leading the way, they came back on deck.

"Jumbo what of the tugboat?" asked Bari King impatiently, as he glanced at Jumbo, who was standing on deck with other men.

"Boss it will soon be here," replied Jumbo, making concerted efforts with his body language to placate Bari King's impatience.

Bari King peeked at the gunboat that escorted the larger boat and felt waves of reassurance. The headlamps of an approaching vessel shone in the distance and prompted Bari King to put on his night vision goggles. He pursed his lips satisfactorily, when he realized that the vessel was his tugboat, employed to tow large barge of bunkered and ill-gotten crude oil to the open Atlantic Ocean, where a tanker operated by Mr. Wong was waiting.

"Mr. Wong, let's go inside," addressed Bari King as he removed the night-vision goggles. Leading the way, he went down and opened the door of a private compartment. Sitting down, he glanced towards Mr. Wong, who sat on an opposite chair.

"The next shipment of goods will arrive Lagos in a month's time," volunteered Mr. Wong.

"I hope there are no hitches," voiced Bari King with a note of concern.

"No! No! Everything is flowing smoothly," replied Mr. Wong.

"Is there any other way we can explore to make our transaction more secure? queried Bari King.

"The current arrangement of taking the crude oil and converting your own share of the proceeds into exportable goods from China is quite okay; we can continue to look at ways of fine tuning the operation," stated Mr. Wong.

"If I think of any new idea that would help; I'II let you know," posited Bari King.

"Okay!" voiced Mr. Wong.

Bari King rose up from his chair and advanced towards the door, with Mr. Wong close to his heels. They came back on deck and beheld Bari King's men as they offloaded the cache of weapons and equipment from the boat.

The night remained an innocent witness to the dark schemes, brewing inside Bari King's mind.

"My friend! I look forward to seeing you again," declared Bari King, as he exchanged warm hugs with Mr. Wong.

"Yes of course and I bid you well," responded Mr. Wong as his slight frame gestured sprightly.

In full view of his men, who labored with the last remnants of the weapons, Bari King disembarked from the boat. His eyes still cloaked with the night-vision goggles, Bari King waved at Mr. Wong and then turned towards his camp. Marveling at the sights, enabled by his night-vision goggles, and in the company of his men, Bari King pounded his legs on the well-worn path that led to his camp.

As they arrived at their camp, its peaceful atmosphere, accompanied by intermittent sounds of insects and carousing animals awakened a longing in Bari King's heart. As he stretched on his bed, without removing his clothes and putting on the light; he longed for the darkness to enshroud his mind and seclude him from the cares of the world. He treasured the peace that overlaid his camp and wondered when his own life would epitomize such serenity.

Inside his tent, Bari King's brisk and sure motions acknowledged the impartiality of the goodness of the morning. He adjusted his black jean trouser and red t- shirt, before promenading out of his tent. Acknowledging greetings from his men, he focused ahead. Five of his men followed suit, as he aligned himself to the path that led to the banks of the river. His footsteps were quick and agile, as he ruminated over the plans that steamed inside his mind. Stepping away from the banks of the river and boarding a waiting launch, they sped off. They arrived at a neighboring village and disembarked at a secluded area spotted by their scout. After traversing a short distance from the banks of the river, they sighted two waiting black Toyota sedans. Acknowledging that the vehicles were theirs, they advanced briskly towards them and boarded. Their surplus shirts and t-shirts concealed powerful pistols that hung over their sides. With Port Harcourt in their minds, they drove off. Some policemen at the various check points that littered Onne Road turned to another direction while others pretended as if they were lacing their boots, as they approached them. Smoothly, they drove into Port Harcourt. They rode into Birabi Street and veered off from it.

"Where are the pictures?" demanded Bari King from the back of the leading vehicle.

The man in the front passenger-seat rapidly opened the pigeonhole and retrieved a bulging manila envelope. Bowing reverentially, he handed the envelope to Bari King.

Bari King smiled mischievously, as he viewed the sexually explicit pictures. He focused his attention on Honorable Kibara's flabby anatomy and pursed his lips sportively.

"I hope he's still there," voiced Bari King, as he communicated to one of his men through his mobile handset.

"Yes master! His girlfriend has left, but he's still in the room," replied the man.

"Hang tight; I'll be there in a jiffy," expressed Bari King.

Driving inside the Guesthouse, they scanned the parking lot. Upon spotting their comrade's vehicle, they drove towards it and parked beside it. Briskly, their comrade alighted from his own vehicle and strode towards them.

"Master he'll soon come down," stated their comrade.

"Is that his vehicle?" asked Bari King through the window, pointing to a well-conditioned Land Cruiser Jeep parked within earshot.

"Yes master," replied the man.

"Does he have any armed orderly?" continued Bari King

"No master; he usually drives himself alone to this place," volunteered the man.

"Good! Very good," enthused Bari King, "You can go back to your vehicle," he directed.

Within Bari King's clear view, Honorable Kibara appeared on the parking lot. Rapidly, Honorable Kibara advanced towards his vehicle. As four vehicles formed a barrier between him and Honorable Kibara, Bari King stealthily emerged from his vehicle and stayed out of Honorable Kibara's view. As the electronic locking system of Honorable Kibara's vehicle sounded, Bari King briskly ambulated from the rear of the Land Cruiser Jeep and tapped Honorable Kibara lightly on the shoulders.

"Who's thahhh! "Ejaculated Honorable Kibara, turning around and fixing eyes dazed by a mixture of dread and surprise on Bari King.

"Surprise! Surprise!" voiced Bari King sportively.

"Bari what are you doing here?" blurted Honorable Kibara in a trembling voice. The corners of his month quivered uncontrollably and betrayed the dread that gnawed at his innards.

"What did you tell your wife when you were leaving the house?" queried Bari King mischievously.

"How do you mean?" asked Honorable Kibara in an unsteady voice filled with apprehension.

"Lock your front door and open the rear one," directed Bari King in an icy tone.

Honorable Kibara quickly obeyed and turned towards Bari King in a meek manner.

"Enter!" commanded Bari King

"As soon as Honorable Kibara's outline disappeared inside his vehicle, Bari King followed suit immediately and closed the door. Shifting uneasily in his chair, Honorable Kibara warily glanced at the brown manila envelope on Bari King's laps.

"Bari you shouldn't be here in Port Harcourt; the police are looking for you and there's a reward on your head," patronized Honorable Kibara.

"Shut up!" barked Bari King, "Since when did you have my interest at heart," snarled Bari King disdainfully.

Abruptly, Honorable Kibara looked away, and the bulging vein across his temple pounded furiously.

"Who's the police?" Voiced Bari King scornfully

Honorable Kibara looked ahead with a faraway expression and forlorn thoughts that wondered where his encounter with Bari King would lead to.

"You went on air and labeled me as an outcast; are you out of your mind? Who is playing the rhythm of destruction that you are gyrating to?" queried Bari King, in a nasty tone. His impatient gestures betrayed a reluctance to restrain himself from inflicting violence.

"Bari take it easy; that statement was meant for public consumption only." His uneasiness steadily rose in intensity.

"So you're now building your public profile at my own expense!" blurted Bari King, with unabated venom.

"Bari I appreciate all you've done for me; without you, my political career would not have taken off," stated Honorable Kibara, still daring not to glance at Bari King.

"I labored with my money and influence to get you elected; what do you think you're trying to do now? If you think that you can jettison me at will and step all over me, in order to further your political career; you've got a storm coming your way," threatened Bari King.

"Bari please don't turn this small issue into a mountain," pleaded Honorable Kibara, flaunting eyes swept by a desperate longing to witness a transformation in Bari King's stormy countenance.

"Small issue?" barked Bari King, "You're calling labeling me as an outcast in public small issue," blurted Bari King with heightened venom.

"Please I'm sorry; I didn't mean to upset you this way," apologized Honorable Kibara.

"Sorry!" Barked Bari King, "all the sorry in this world will not deter me from what I have to do," voiced Bari King angrily.

Slightly stooping under the weighty mixture of fear and gloom, Honorable Kibara opened his mouth to talk but words failed him.

"Do you know what is inside this envelope?" asked Bari King

with a mischievous smile, as he raised the envelope to Honourable Kibara's view.

At the sight of the envelope, Honorable Kibara's mind sank into an endless abyss, and he felt his energy speedily draining away. He nursed an ominous feeling about the envelope.

Opening the envelope and retrieving a glossy picture card from it, he leisurely tossed the card on Honorable Kibara's laps. Taking one look at the picture, Honourable Kibara veered away abruptly from it and cupped his face with the palm of his right hand. As he shook his head despondently, a myriad of confusing and hopeless thoughts raced inside his mind. The image of himself in a compromising posture with his nude mistress got stuck in his mind. The scandalous image assailed him with oppressive feelings that squeezed at the pit of his stomach.

"How did you get that picture?" stammered Honorable Kibara, afraid to take a second glance at the picture.

"How do you think your wife will react to this picture?" posed Bari King, broadening his mischievous smile.

"Please don't go there!" blurted Honorable Kibara with driving urgency.

"What will the public think about you now?" quipped Bari King.

"What is the business of the public with that damn picture?" cried Honorable Kibara desperately.

"They need to know what their favorite House of Assembly member is up to," stated Bari King remorselessly.

"Bari please don't finish me," blurted Honorable Kibara in a plaintive tone, gazing at Bari King with a woebegone expression.

"You are the architect of your own doom," stated Bari King.

"But you won't gain anything by circulating that picture," voiced Honorable Kibara, in a pleading tone that failed to move Bari King.

"If you don't want me to circulate this picture, you must quickly get back on air and eat every word you mouthed against me," averred Bari King.

Placing his sweaty palms against his forehead and covering his eyes, Honorable Kibara shook his head helplessly. He drew in a deep breath and exhaled loudly.

"If you hesitate to comply, I'll start with your wife," threatened Bari King with a taunting laughter.

Glancing weakly at Bari King, Honorable Kibara was rendered speechless by his despair.

"You can have the picture for company," derided Bari King with laughter. He alighted smartly from Honorable Kibara's vehicle, without bothering to close the door.

Boarding his own vehicle, Bari King still tolerated a mischievous grin on his face. Longing for the peace and safety of their encampment, Bari King reclined on his seat, as they sped off.

The morning, clad with a cheerful light, was the only witness as Bari King sat opposite Akoju, his medicine man.

"You'll provide me with some money to buy the goat and other items required for the full moon ritual," began Akoju.

"That is settled," reassured Bari King.

"I'll make the ritual as potent as possible now that you're preparing for an assault," stated Akoju.

"I trust what you can do," lauded Bari King.

Akoju smiled and adjusted his bracelet, made of cowry shells.

"There's something more I want you to do for me; I have a white man here," disclosed Bari King.

"I've heard about that," replied Akoju.

"I want you to frighten the living daylight out of him." Bari King's mischievous grin offered further encouragement to Akoju.

"Don't worry about that," stated Akoju with an impish grin.

Bari King led the way, and they ambled out of his tent. At a safe distance, Bari King observed Akoju as he casually unwound the coils of a medium-sized python from a nearby orange tree.

With Bari King in front, they advanced towards Mr. Gerard's tent.

"Open this tent," barked Bari King, as he stood in front of it and absentmindedly waved at his men in response to their greetings.

Unzipping the door of the tent, Mr. Gerard stepped aside with great unease. Bari King entered the tent and stood at its extreme right. With shoulders hung with the python, Akoju made his entrance and presented a sight that forced Mr. Gerard to reel backwards in fright. With features drained of their vitality, Mr. Gerard managed to stabilize himself. His motions desperate, he glanced at Bari King and then at Akoju. The desperate look in his eyes failed to deter Bari King from initiating the rest of his plans. With trembling hands and a riotous mind, Mr. Gerard adjusted his loose fitting trousers, tightly held around his waist with a leather belt. An overwhelming sense of foreboding gripped him and prevented him from turning away from the slithering tongue of the python.

Betraying no emotion, Bari King brandished his satellite phone.

"You people are toying with the life of your man," voiced Bari King coldly as he rightfully positioned the phone.

"Putting the gold bullion together is proving to be quite difficult; why can't we settle with money?" came the entreating voice from the other end.

Removing the phone from his ears, Bari King turned towards Akoju; with an outstretched hand, he goaded him towards Mr. Gerard. His hands still lowered, Bari King ignored the barely audible words, emanating from his phone. The leering smile mirrored by Akoju's countenance and the slithering tongue of the python conspired together and rendered Mr. Gerard's temple balmy with fear. Akoju advanced mercilessly towards Mr. Gerard with ill intentions.

5

Mr. Gerard's heartbeat became one with the unbridled rhythm of fear. He shrank backwards with awkward steps and tripped against his mattress.

"Please get him away from me," entreated Mr. Gerard desperately, in a quivering tone. He dared not to shift his gaze away from Akoju and his serpent.

"Your people don't care about you; why should I care," blurted Bari King, as he ambled towards Mr. Gerard with an outstretched right hand, still clutching his phone. He clearly intended for the man at the other end of the line to readily perceive Mr. Gerard's fearful protests and squeals.

"I will do anything; just get him away from me," wailed Mr. Gerard, as he struggled to drag himself up from the mattress. Cornered at the rear of his tent and trembling with fear, Mr. Gerard gazed at Akoju with unblinking eyes as the distance that separated them diminished.

"Akoju!" called Bari King.

At the sound of his name, Akoju halted in his tracks and turned backwards towards Bari King. A look of disappointment reigned over the features of Akoju's countenance, and his mind was forced to shelve the countless malevolent schemes he had already devised against Mr. Gerard. Turning towards Mr. Gerard, he grinned maleficently.

"Lady Luck will not smile on you next time," voiced Bari King, as he gazed coldly at Mr. Gerard.

Motioning for Akoju to retreat from Mr. Gerard's position, he lifted his phone to his ears.

"Did you hear your man screaming?" asked Bari King in an emotionless tone.

"What are you doing to him?" replied the voice from the other end of the line.

"What I'm doing to him is not your business; your business is to raise the gold bullions I asked for, before I do something worse to him," threatened Bari King, as he abruptly cut off the line.

"You are not better-of dead; you will not know any peace if your remains are buried inside this African soil, so you better pray for your people to come up with what I asked for." Bari King's frosty and merciless tone instigated another round of goose bumps across Mr. Gerard's frame.

Turning away from Mr. Gerard, Bari King headed towards the threshold of the tent with Akoju and his serpentine companion in tow.

The morning was becoming nostalgic, as Bari King sat on an easy chair inside his tent and absentmindedly focused on the active screen of the television set. His mind was troubled by a newly received piece of information. He picked up his satellite phone and punched in some numbers.

"So you have now aligned yourself with Power Donga?" began Bari King in an acidic tone.

"Why would I do that?" replied Honorable Kibara in a stressed voice.

"You tell me," voiced Bari King with a very hard edge to his voice.

"Bari! You know that we have a special relationship." The tautness in his voice betrayed the fear that gripped him.

"You should know better than sweet-talking me," admonished Bari King sternly.

"I am not in league with Power Donga." His vehement denial failed to alter Bari King's thoughts.

"My sources are reliable," interjected Bari King.

"They are wrong this time around," stated Honorable Kibara, in a tone that sought to convince Bari King.

"I know why you are conspiring with Power Donga; is it not about those compromising photographs of you and your mistress that I have in my possession? You would be very glad to see me neutralized," articulated Bari King with a sardonic smile.

"Eh! eh! em! Thoughts of those pictures make me nervous; I admit that; I also want you to know that I have not lost my senses; why would I endanger my life by plotting against you." His tone flaunted his renewed resolve to convince Bari King.

"I'm not convinced by your words and tone of voice; I know that my sources are correct," restated Bari King

"Please listen to me; don't take any punitive action against me yet; I know that you don't waste time in matters like this," entreated Honorable Kibara desperately

"Your pleas are coming rather late; severe punitive actions have already been set in motion; you will pay a bitter price for plotting against me," voiced Bari King in an implacable tone.

"Bari please don't do this to me," implored Honorable Kibara.

The click of the phone against Honorable Kibara's ears signaled the end of the exchange, as Bari King impolitely cut off the line.

Gently dropping his satellite phone on a nearby table, he reached out for his short wave radio set and summoned Jumbo to his tent.

"Boss I'm here," stated Jumbo, as he stood before the threshold of Bari King's tent.

"Come right in," beckoned Bari King.

"Tomorrow morning, you will initiate all the actions that I outlined against Honorable Kibara; do not fail me," charged Bari King as he gazed intently at Jumbo.

"Everything will happen according to how you planned it; I will proceed to Port Harcourt right away," assured Jumbo.

"Okay!" stated Bari King, nodding his head in agreement.

As Jumbo promenaded away from him, a mischievous grin crossed his face. With full awareness of his brutal plans, he tried to imagine the resultant expression that would adorn Honorable Kibara's face.

Rising up from the chair, Bari King stretched himself on his mattress and closed his eyes. Myriad of thoughts crowded his mind, but one particular thought reared its head above the others. Thoughts about his future and survival gripped him and refused to let go. He wondered how his future would turn out, if indeed he survived long enough. He was torn between his desire for a peaceful family life and his craving for the commanding power that he welded over his men. He made serious attempts to mentally convince himself that his desire for the good of his people far outweighed his drive for the material things that came with his position. In the end, he pulled his bed sheet over his head and entreated sleep to rescue him from his inner turmoil.

The air-conditioned air soothingly caressed Honourable Kibara, as if it knew about the damning events that were already unfolding. He reclined inside his chauffeur-driven Toyota Land Cruiser SUV and cast imperious glances at the scenes that flitted past him. With a great measure of personal satisfaction, he observed the lead-vehicle in his convoy. Its flashing amber lights and blaring siren tremendously uplifted his personal pride and ego. As they drove along Forces Avenue, his convoy, with reckless abandon, abruptly veered into an adjacent lane, against the normal run of traffic, in a bid to escape a mild and tolerable traffic challenge. The screeching tyres and alarmed expressions of law-abiding and oncoming motorists only elicited a haughty grin from his face. Honourable Kibara considered the brazen show of power as part of the perks of his office as the speaker of the State House of Assembly. He paid little attention to the helpless and lawful motorists swept to the roadside by his convoy. He focused his mind on the issues that would define the upcoming conference of speakers of State Houses of Assemblies, scheduled to commence in twenty-five minute's time at Hotel Presidential. He appraised his dark Italian suit together with the matching pair of shoes and shook his head with an air of satisfaction. He adjudged his attire quite befitting for the office of the Chairman.

As his driver maneuvered into the parking lot, Honourable Kibara frowned at the rowdy scene that prevailed on the lobby that led into the conference hall. He wondered what his colleagues, who were invited to join the speakers, were doing outside, instead of being seated and prepared for the business of the day. They broke up into crowds of varying numbers and emotively interacted in a verbal manner.

Instructively, Honourable Kibara arrested his motions and sat up on his chair, as a colleague approached him. He read the pensive expression nurtured by the man and concluded that all was not well.

"Something is not right, out there sir," ejaculated the man as he pointed towards the direction of the conference hall.

"What exactly is the matter?" asked Honourable Kibara, with a racing heartbeat, as he gazed into the man's face through the unobstructed window of his vehicle.

"Sir! Can I talk to you privately," requested his colleague in a subdued tone. His sober demeanor heightened Honourable Kibara's sense of foreboding.

"Sure!" replied Honourable Kibara, "please give us some room," he demanded authoritatively, as he glanced at his driver and police orderly.

"Yes Sir!" they chorused as they hastened out of the car.

With a clear view of his colleague entering his vehicle, he propelled the tinted glass of his window back into position.

"Something bad is happening out there sir," continued the man as he sat up inside the vehicle.

"What exactly is it?" queried Honourable Kibara with tones of impatience.

"I don't know how to begin sir," blurted the man in a strained voice.

"Just tell me what's bloody going on," snapped Honourable Kibara impatiently.

"Nude and compromising pictures of you and a certain woman are circulating inside the conference hall," ejaculated the man with clear signs of difficulty.

"What! Eeh! Em! Em!" muttered Honourable Kibara unin-telligibly, as he collapsed against the seat of his vehicle. His chest heaved violently up and down. His temples together with his forehead broke out in tepid perspiration despite the cool ambience of the vehicle.

"How?" he managed mournfully after some seconds.

"We discovered the pictures when we arrived here this morning; lots of them were scattered in the conference hall," volunteered the man sympathetically.

"Heee! Heee! I'm finished," lamented Honourable Kibara.

"Sir, it was difficult to contain the situation; the pictures were just too many," stated the man regretfully.

"What of the other Speakers? Did any of them see the pictures?" asked Honourable Kibara, nursing a very fragile ray of hope.

"I'm afraid sir; some of them did see the pictures," disclosed the man.

As his midsection buckled gracelessly, Honourable Kibara supported his forehead with the palm of his right hand.

"What of our colleagues? Did a large section of them see the photographs?" managed Honourable Kibara in a drained voice, without raising his head.

"I'm afraid again," replied the man.

"Hee! Hee! Hee! This is the end of me," rued Honourable Kibara.

"Sir I strongly advise that you turn away and leave this premises," stated the man.

"Everything is finished, Hee! Hee! Hee!" moaned Honourable Kibara as he shook his hung down head dejectedly.

Quietly, the man opened the door of the vehicle and stepped out. Honourable Kibara, still consumed by despair, was oblivious of the sound emitted by the door, as it closed after the man. Some minutes after the man exited the vehicle, Honourable Kibara raised his head and managed to inject some composure into his motions. Lowering the glass of a nearby window, he beckoned on his driver and orderly.

"Just drive out of this place without the convoy," directed Honourable Kibara in a firm voice, as he gazed at his driver.

"Yes sir, which way should I go?" asked the driver.

"Enter Aba Road, I'll give you further directions," stated Honourable Kibara. His composed exterior masked a mind, plagued by confusion and turmoil. He was unsure of where to go and his throat was parched by thirst, occasioned by severe hopelessness. Thinking of home, he wondered if his wife had come in possession of the photographs. The mere thought of his wife together with the photographs made his stomach to rumble oppressively, as he attained new levels of despair. He strongly suspected that his wife must be stoking up a blaze, waiting to consume his peace and sense of wellbeing, at home. He decided against home and his office. In accordance with his directives, his driver drove aimlessly into GRA Phase II. Reasoning with himself, he decided not to postpone the day of reckoning with his wife any longer. Mentally acknowledging himself, his driver and police orderly, he counseled himself wisely. Sadly, he wondered how life without his convoy and perks of his position would look like. He didn't expect things to come abruptly to an end so soon. The street scenes that drew the full brunt of the pride, bestowed by his temporal position, now humbled him. He strongly suspected that his days as Speaker of the state legislature were indeed numbered.

"Take me home," directed Honourable Kibara with an air of resignation.

As the driver detoured towards his residence, he closed his eyes and began to brace himself up.

"You can all go," addressed Honourable Kibara as the vehicle parked inside his compound.

"Okay sir," chorused the driver and police orderly.

Advancing towards the main building, he observed with a mild sense of relief, that his wife's vehicle was not present in the premises. A domestic servant opened the door as he approached its threshold. Noncommittally nodding his head to the servant's greeting, he ambled straight to the master bedroom. The controlled expression on his face began to show cracks as he turned the door knob. He collapsed on the bed, without undressing. With enervated motions, he stretched forth his hand and switched on the air-conditioning unit. Rolling about helplessly on the bed and eventually facing down, he placed his right hand against his chest and felt its violent pounding. The minutes steadily passed him by without his awareness.

The blaring of horn outside his premises jolted him from his woeful reverie. An overcast of the strongest foreboding suddenly gripped the atmosphere of the bedroom. The familiar sound of the horn announced his wife's homecoming to him. He sat up on the bed and glanced about himself like a caged animal. His acute awareness soaked in the sound of the vehicle as it was maneuvered into the premises. The sound generated by the vehicle's door, as it was opened and closed, heightened his anxiety. With motions, stiffened by woebegone feelings, he gaped at the door knob. Honourable Kibara lowered his head as the door knob turned violently.

"So what is the meaning of these pictures?" queried his wife angrily, as she banged the door mindlessly and displayed a brown manila envelope before her husband, "So you've been whoring about town, without any regard for me or the children," continued his wife, as she threw the envelope at him and advanced menacingly towards him.

Hemmed- in by the damning photographs, spilled on the floor, and his wife's unrestrained wrath, Honourable Kibara felt an oppressive tautness in the pit of his stomach.

"You are not talking now; I bet you were not speechless, when you were in bed with that whore," voiced his wife disgustingly as she stood before him.

With enfeebled motions, Honourable Kibara lifted his head. He opened his mouth to talk but nothing came out. The subdued expression on his face failed to temper the blazing anger that flashed in his wife's eyes. Disengaging his eye contact with his wife, he lowered his head again.

"May be this will make you talk," barked his wife as she slapped him heavily across the face.

He reeled briefly from the impact of his wife's physical assault and steadied himself. Still numbed by the events of the day, he proffered no reaction.

"Can you imagine what you have done to me and the children," blurted his wife as her apparel danced to the tune of her wrath.

Languorously, Honourable Kibara rose up from the bed and focused at the door.

"Where are you going to?" snapped his wife as she glared at her husband's departing outline. Her indignation, knowing no bounds and plaguing her with confusion, rooted her to a spot.

With spiritless motions, he opened the door and walked out of the room. He focused his attention towards the direction of their guestroom. Glad that his children were not present to witness the shameful drama between him and his wife, he sat down on a chair inside the guestroom and cupped his jaw with the palm of his right hand. He turned towards the bulge in the pocket of his trouser as his phone began to ring. Retrieving the phone, he glanced at it and suspected the caller to be Bari King. He mentally debated with himself whether to answer the phone or not. Moping morosely into space, he decided to take the call.

"Honourable how is your day going?" voiced Bari King with a mischievous laughter.

"What have you done to me?" blurted Honourable Kibara in a plaintive voice.

"What did I do?" taunted Bari King.

"You know what you did with the pictures," responded Honourable Kibara accusingly.

"Nobody crosses me and lives to tell a pleasant tale; you had to learn the hard way," vaunted Bari King. The click of the phone against Honourable Kibara's ears informed him that Bari King had abruptly cut-off the line. Still holding the phone against his ears, Honourable Kibara bored cluelessly into space.

The afternoon was about to realize its full potentials, as Bari King stirred on his mattress. He sat up on the mattress and rubbed his eyes leisurely. The familiar sound of birds and animals that populated the rainforest held his attention captive. The high pitched calls of the Colubus monkeys stirred him deeply and intuitively reopened a deep wound inside his consciousness. In addition, a desperate yearning possessed his soul. Unable to reduce his yearning into thoughts and words, he still convinced himself that something was missing in his life. He glanced about himself, in search of a palliative preoccupation that would distract him from his deep and mysterious longing.

"Boss! Akoju is here," came the voice of one of his men, outside his tent.

"Akoju?" muttered Bari King softly to himself. Reaching out for a nearby t-shirt that hung on a chair, he stood up. "Let him in," directed Bari King loudly, as he began to rid his face of the frowns instigated by Akoju's coming.

"I wasn't expecting you so soon," voiced Bari King with a blank expression.

"Something came up," responded Akoju, as he sat opposite Bari King.

"Something like what?" asked Bari King with a sardonic smile.

"I need to fortify the protection ritual for you and your men; and secondly, I lost my father," narrated Akoju.

"But you received enough money for your rituals," stated Bari King.

"Like I said; I need to fortify the rituals because of what lies ahead of you, and I would be grateful for any support for my father's burial," averred Akoju patiently.

"I've never really tested the efficacy of your medicine, because I've never been shot," voiced Bari King with a sportive grin.

"That is part of the medicine," defended Akoju.

"What of the men that I lost?" asked Bari King attentively.

"They simply disobeyed the rules and rituals of the medicine," explained Akoju, as he gestured confidently with his lean frame.

"If your medicine is that strong, it should have prevented your father from dying?" queried Bari King, as he broadened his sportive grin.

"Bari, I too have my own limits," replied Akoju as he shook his head incredulously.

"You'll get more money," promised Bari King with a benign smile

"And my father's burial?" presented Akoju with an entreating look.

"You'll get some support for that too," assured Bari King.

"Thank you very much; may the great spirits continue to protect you," stated Akoju gratefully.

Having acknowledged Akoju's gratitude with graceful nods of his head, he courteously turned away from him.

Acknowledging the activity in his camp together with the guns and ammunitions, through the window of his tent, he wondered if his life would ever become normal again.

The vibration of his satellite phone interrupted his heartfelt reverie, and he reached out for it.

"Bari it's me," came the voice from the other end of the line.

"Officer, how are you today?" asked Bari King leisurely.

"I'm okay," responded the man.

"So what gives today?" continued Bari King in a robust tone.

"I just want to inform you that the Joint Task Force is beefing up their troop formation in your village; a lot of plainclothes intelligence officers will be joining in," revealed the officer.

"Uh....huh," blurted Bari King distastefully.

"Well, I've done my own bit; the rest is up to you; I trust that you know what to do," voiced the man.

"Your JTF does not frighten me," vaunted Bari King.

"This is not the police only," sounded the man with a note of caution.

"Like I said my feet are solidly on the ground," stated Bari King firmly.

"There's another thing: my wife recently delivered a baby boy; you know how difficult things are in the country," intimated the officer.

"What is this? Is this a ploy to squeeze out more money from me; you should be satisfied with what I pay you for your information; it is about five times of what they pay you in the police force," ejaculated Bari King with abhorrence, as he cut-off the line abruptly.

He paced vigorously to and fro in his tent, in a bid to neutralize his sour feelings and uplift his mood.

"Boss it's me," sounded Jumbo outside Bari King's tent.

"Come in," responded Bari King.

"Walking respectfully into the tent, Jumbo stood before Bari King.

"Boss I discovered something," enthused Jumbo.

"What is it?" queried Bari King, as he parted his eyelids impatiently.

"I've just learnt about a certain medicine man; they say his medicine is impenetrable," narrated Jumbo with eyes that glowed in awe.

Bari King smiled appreciatively and sat down on a chair.

"So where is this medicine man?" asked Bari King with keen interest.

"Eeh! Em! Sorry Boss; in my excitement, I forgot to ask about the location of the medicine man's abode, but I'll get on to it right away," stated Jumbo apologetically

"You do that and get back to me immediately," directed Bari King.

"Yes Boss," responded Jumbo, turning away from him.

Rising from the chair, Bari King ambled leisurely to the window. The sight of the green foliage of trees, dancing freely in mid-air, bruised the yearning of his heart.

The cool ambience of Bari King's tent was grateful for the morning's benevolence.

"Do you now have information about the whereabouts of this medicine man?" queried Bari King, as he gazed expectantly at Jumbo.

"Yes Boss," replied Jumbo.

"Is it very far from here?" continued Bari King.

"His village is not very far from here; it is in Ibani town," revealed Jumbo.

"I've heard of the town. Tomorrow, we're going to saddle up and head straight for the town; go and get the men and equipment ready," commanded Bari King.

"Yes Boss," replied Jumbo as he bowed slightly in a respectful gesture.

Forest sounds, concocted by birds and monkeys, formed an upbeat background. Bari King and his men strode fearlessly across the floor of the forest. They presented a fearsome sight with their shoulders hung with magazines of bullets. Semi-automatic and automatic weapons dangled by their sides and bolstered their confidence. Stepping onto the banks of Kino

River, they briskly boarded waiting white launches that boasted of machine guns. Feeling his pistol under his red t-shirt, he gestured his medium-built frame confidently. After about fifty-five minutes, a jetty loomed before them, and they approached it with heightened vigilance. Upon sighting the armed band, local fishermen paddled away from them in a hurry. Prospective commuters, waiting for their turns on the banks of the River, tactfully melted away in different directions. Their coming instigated a climate of fear that oppressed the jetty and its environs. Passers-by cast wary glances at them and scurried away. Anchoring their boats, Bari King and his men promptly alighted from them. Some of his men glanced about with arrogant airs and reveled in the climate of insecurity they brought upon the people. As Jumbo advanced towards a near-by clique of men, some of them broke away and walked briskly away, while others remained rooted at a spot, unable to free themselves from the devitalizing fear that gripped them. They darted apprehensive glances at Jumbo and wondered about the nature of his mission.

"Relax I just want to ask for directions," began Jumbo in a reassuring tone.

The men nodded cautiously in acknowledgement.

"We are looking for Agila, the great medicine man," continued Jumbo as he focused on one of the men.

"His place is not far from the town square; just follow that road and ask again, when you reach the town square," replied the man, as he pointed to the main road opposite the jetty.

"Thank you," volunteered Jumbo, turning away.

Waiting expectantly, Bari King focused at Jumbo, as he approached him.

"So did you get the right directions?" asked Bari King.

"Yes Boss, we need to start on that road," stated Jumbo,

standing before Bari King and pointing at the main road.

Striding briskly along the road, Bari King and his men paid little attention to the passersby, who paused abruptly on their tracks with terror-stricken expressions.

"Please we are looking for Agila, the great medicine man," asked Jumbo, standing in front of a stranger.

"Take the next right turn and stop at the fifth house," hurriedly replied the man. He scurried away before Jumbo could offer any gratitude for his help.

Glancing at the nearby town square, Jumbo detoured to the right with Bari King and the rest of their comrades in tow.

Mud houses with thatched roofs lined the dirt road that hosted their vigorous footsteps. A flock of swallows, on a neighboring Iroko tree, suddenly let out a plaintive cry and took flight, as if in protest to the armed visitors' intrusion.

"Boss I believe this is the house," stated Jumbo, standing before a mud house and gazing at Bari King.

"I'm going in alone; find a convenient place and wait," voiced Bari King, marching along the side of the mud house.

Entering the compound through a side pedestrian gate, constructed of rough timber battens, he failed to encounter a soul. A grotto of sorts constructed of mud walls and thatched roof tugged at his attention, and he ambled cautiously towards it. He noticed a string of fresh lemon grass supported by the door posts. Peering heedfully inside the grotto, he defined a rattle, made of bamboo stems and adorned with cowry shells, and an assortment of herbs tied up in neat bundles. Staring at the raised mud-based platform that supported the items, he cocked his head thoughtfully.

"Stranger! How may I help you?" came a genial male voice from behind.

Recovering his composure, Bari King swung around swiftly.

"Are you in the habit of poking your nose into other people's affairs?" continued the man, still wearing a genial smile.

"Please pardon my rudeness; my curiosity got the better part of me," replied Bari King apologetically.

"So what brings you to my quarters?" continued the man as he focused intently at Bari King.

"May your countenance greet more mornings; I'm here to see Agila, the great medicine man," stated Bari King courteously.

"What about?" queried the man with a curious glint in his eyes.

"Something tells me that you are Agila," blurted Bari King as he broadened his smile

"So!?" voiced the man.

"Your reputation as a medicine man is quite renowned; I need your help," expressed Bari King.

"What is your name?" queried the man calmly, as he adjusted the wrapper, tied about his slender waist.

"They call me Bari King." The sportive glint in his eyes did not ruffle the man's calmness.

"That name sounds familiar; Uh....huh, I remember now, you are part of the group the Government labels as militants," voiced the man without betraying any emotion.

"I'm a freedom fighter; the interest of our people is uppermost in my mind," uttered Bari King defensively.

"Are you sure about that?" stated the man doubtfully.

"Surely, you must have heard about my charitable deeds," stated Bari King with an air of pride.

"Compare that with the amount you pocket," articulated the man with a slight hint of scorn.

"What do you mean by that?" blurted Bari King, as his eyes flashed angrily. '' You should direct that statement at the Federal Government; they are the ones that sell all our crude oil and leave us with nothing; I have lifted some people out of poverty, and that is something," continued Bari King.

"Don't forget that we have sons and daughters, who are in Port Harcourt, looking for jobs that they can't find, because of your kind. The violent and lawless activities of militants have driven many companies from our land, and others are downsizing their activities. Tell me! How does that make you a hero?" aired the man in a tone that sought to provoke some contemplation in the mind of his visitor.

"On which side are you on .... Old man?" blurted Bari King, as he leaned menacingly towards the man.

"What are you going to do? Hurt me? Do you see any fear in my eyes?" voiced the man, in a composed tone, still maintaining eye contact with Bari King.

"I still need your help; I have many enemies; criminals who are worse than me," uttered Bari King with a frank smile.

"I assume that you are referring to your fellow militants. We have heard stories about the wanton rape, bullying, and murders committed by your kind," continued the man in steady voice.

"I am certain that you have heard about me; I don't condone the vices you mentioned," uttered Bari King vehemently

"Can you deny that you don't have blood on your hands?" stated the man with a knowing smile.

"I protect myself," asserted Bari King.

"Well I am Agila, herbalist and healer, I don't do the kind of medicine that you're looking for," expressed the man with a genial smile, "you can come and sit down and share some homemade gin with me if you wish; that is the best I can offer you," continued Agila as he ambled towards nearby and roughhewn table and chairs.

Bari King trailed after him and sat opposite him

"Kasi please bring my drink," beckoned Agila, as he gently stroked his bare upper frame.

"Father I'll be along shortly," rang Kasi's voice from the direction of the main building.

Kasi appeared from the main building with an enamel tray, laden with a bottle of homemade gin and two serving glasses.

"Good morning sir," greeted Kasi as she set the tray down on the table and threw a fleeting and respectful glance at Bari King

"Good morning to you too," reciprocated Bari King courteously.

Agile poured some of the drink into his glass and then turned towards Bari King.

"Please don't pour too much; I'm not much of a drinker," stated Bari King.

"My daughter Kasi- we struggled very hard to put her through school, and she is a graduate now. As a matter of fact, she is finding it very difficult to get any job now, because of the activities of you and your kind," uttered Agila calmly.

"I'm not the cause of your daughter's unemployment," replied Bari King with an amusing smile, "the Federal Government is to blame ," continued Bari King.

"I see" voiced Agila incredulously.

"If the Government is fair to us, your daughter may not even need to look for job; the money we would be realizing from our own share of crude oil proceeds would be quit substantial," continued Bari King in a stimulated tone.

"Is that what you are fighting for: to stay at home and be receiving money from Government, that is not self-respecting at all," stated Agila, nodding his head emphatically.

"I'm fighting to make life easier for our people," responded Bari King in a level tone.

"But you're ending up making it worse for them," countered

Agila defiantly.

"Anyways............. Let me not deviate from my main reason for coming here; I need medicine for protection," voiced Bari King thoughtfully.

"I'm sorry; I don't have what you need," reiterated Agila.

"I can provide you with money that can change the lives of you and your family," proposed Bari King in a conspiratorial tone.

"Ah...........ha, I suspected that everything will boil down to money; I'm happy with the contentment in my heart; your money can not add to it," replied Agila with a firm air of conviction.

"Are you sure about that?" responded Bari King with a sportive grin, "if you don't want it, your family might need it," he continued.

"Leave my family out of this," defended Agila.

"I made my inquiries very well; and I know that I'm in the right place; you haven't seen the last of me," voiced Bari King in a determined tone as he stood up.

Agila smiled and shook his head in a disapproving manner. Bari King smiled back at him and walked briskly out of the compound. Standing in front of Agila's compound, Bari King gazed at his men, as they hurried towards him from the shade of a nearby Iroko tree, across the road.

"We are staying put here; go and arrange for accommodation and cook," directed Bari King as he focused on Jumbo

"Boss! Opigo is from here, and he has a building that we can use," intimated Jumbo.

"Opigo, why didn't you say that you are from here?" asked Bari King with a genial smile as he gazed at Opigo.

"Nothing Boss," replied Opigo calmly.

"Do you know Agila, the medicine man?" continued Bari King

"Boss, I didn't really grow up here," stated Opigo as he adjusted the magazine of bullets that hung across his shoulder.

"Let's head to your place; I hope you'll host us well," voiced Bari King sportively.

Opigo led the; way and they briskly progressed away from the vicinity of Agila's residence. As they approached the town square, some of the townsfolk strained their necks to have a peek at them; while others hurried away in opposite direction. Their brazen and bold airs added a twist of danger to the erstwhile sleepy town.

"You have done well here," enthused Bari King as he crossed the threshold of Opigo's bungalow, one of the few sandcrete block houses in the town.

"Thank you Boss," replied Opigo, with an appreciative smile, "the master bedroom is for you," continued Opigo as he smiled respectfully at Bari King. "Go and get it ready now," commanded Opigo, turning towards his younger brother.

The morning's benevolence was still ambling along the course ordained for it by nature. Bari King lay on the bed, and his thoughts continued to search for a means of getting Agila to co-operate with him. Unable to make any breakthrough in his search, he alighted from the bed and advanced towards the door.

Sitting behind the dining table, he stared absentmindedly at the steaming plate of jollof rice and fried fish. Their combined aroma failed to ensnare his senses.

"Jumbo!" bellowed Bari King

"Yes Boss," replied Jumbo as he hurried towards him from a nearby room.

"Go and locate the residence of their traditional ruler," directed Bari King, without looking in his direction.

"Right away Boss," voiced Jumbo, briskly turning away.

Whirling towards that food, he shoveled some spoonfuls of rice into his mouth. His inattentiveness prevented him from savoring the good taste of the food.

Pacing up and down inside the living room, Bari King impatiently glanced intermittently at his wrist watch.

"Have you located the place?" asked Bari King in a clean voice as Jumbo entered the living room

"Yes Boss," replied Jumbo, closing the door.

"Is he in now?" continued Bari King

"Yes Boss," stated Jumbo.

"We are going to see him right away," dictated Bari King, hurriedly sitting down and tying the lace of his canvass shoes.

Bari King, in the company of seven of his men, armed with AK-47 assault rifles and corresponding magazines advanced towards the palace of the traditional ruler. Their train still attracted wary and apprehensive looks from passersby.

Without any challenge, they entered the palace of the traditional ruler. The bungalow constructed of sandcrete blocks was an ill-maintained affair with peeling paint.

"We are here to see his royal highness," voiced Jumbo, as he gazed at an approaching teenager.

"I'll go and inform him," replied the hesitant teenager as he hurried away from them.

Bari King glanced about the poverty beaten ambience of the palace and shook his head introspectively.

"So....how may I help you," began the paramount ruler as he peered curiously at Bari King.

"Bari King," uttered Bari King, expecting the man's eyes to light up with recognition.

"I've heard about you, but I wonder what my village has to offer you," stated the man languorously.

"Let's talk privately; I have some interesting propositions," coaxed Bari King.

"Okay," replied the man, yawning tiredly.

The untidy gray that clothed the man's hair and beard highlighted his lean physicality. Bari King trailed after him, as he led the way; while his men advanced towards a nearby windowless communal hall.

"Please sit down," beckoned the paramount ruler, pointing to a neighbouring rusty metal chair.

"Thank you," expressed Bari King, sitting down.

"I wonder what you want from me; as you can see; I don't have much to offer," stated the man in a disinterested manner; as he sat opposite Bari King.

"I'm about to change all that," asserted Bari King with a smile.

"How?" enquired the man with a curious stare

"Chief, I'll make you a rich man if you help me out," proposed Bari King with an imperious smile.

"Chief Domre!" voiced the man, as he introduced himself, "and what kind of help are you seeking for?" asked Chief Domre keenly, as he adjusted his yellowing white singlet.

"If you can get Agila to provide me with some of his potent and protective medicine, I'll do big things for you," continued Bari King.

"Ah.....haaa! I knew it would be a tough one," expressed Chief Domre in a disappointed tone as he reclined on his chair.

"What is tough about my request?" queried Bari King.

"Agila is a principled medicine man; I've not known him to compromise for the sake of money; if he wants to do it, he'll do it; if he doesn't want to do it, he won't do it; he is as simple as that," stated Chief Domre.

"But you're the paramount ruler here; you must have a way of getting him to do your bidding," articulated Bari King with a tinge of anxiety.

"If it does not go against his principles," replied Chief Domre.

"Who does he think he is?" blurted Bari King angrily.

"He must be something; for you to come here, looking for him," uttered Chief Domre in a sassy tone.

"If you get him to co-operate with me, I'll refurbish your palace and enrich your pocket with one million naira," offered Bari King.

"There may be a way, if you're willing to co-operate; medicine craft runs in their lineage; Agila took an oath to protect the paramount ruler and his family," stated Chief Domre.

"I can't see how that affects me," voiced Bari King as he shrugged his shoulders.

"If you agree to marry one of my daughters, you will become part of my family, and he won't have any choice but to prepare the protective medicine for you," continued Chief Domre, nursing a conspiratorial smile.

"What!" ejaculated Bari King.

6

Shifting uneasily on his chair, Bari King appraised the daring grin on Chief Domre's face.

"Marry your daughter?" uttered Bari King incredulously.

"Yes! That may be the only way," continued Chief Domre, undeterred by Bari King's reaction.

"Huh..... huh..... huh! I don't think its possible," uttered Bari King.

"Why not? You haven't even seen my daughter," persisted Chief Domre.

"Chief, forget about that," expressed Bari King as he shook his head doubtfully.

"Yena, bring drink for me and our visitor; bring the dry gin," beckoned Chief Domre, turning away from Bari King and peering at the main building.

Yena, emerging shortly with an ill-conditioned enamel tray, laden with a bottle of dry gin and two glasses, approached her father and Bari King.

"Good morning Sir," greeted Yena, as she cast a fleeting glance at Bari King and set the tray on a coarse metal table, between Bari King and her father.

"Good morning to you too," responded Bari King pleasantly.

"Do you still think that my daughter is not worth your while?" voiced Chief Domre with an impish grin.

"Chief, I don't mean any offence, your daughter is tall, dark and beautiful, but marriage is the last thing on my mind right now; I'm sure you'll understand that," stated Bari King calmly.

"Do you want me to call her out again, so that you can have a second look?" posed Chief Domre.

"Chief that won't be necessary," objected Bari King.

"Are you sure about that?" proffered Chief Domre.

"Chief, let's get back to the issue at hand, somebody will bring one hundred thousand naira to you, and when you find another way of getting Agila to co-operate with me, you'll get the rest of what I promised you," stated Bari King as he stood up.

"I'm telling you that marrying my daughter is the easiest way of getting Agila to co-operate with you," reiterated Chief Domre.

"Surely there must be another way; find it; ummh! I don't have much time on my hands here," expressed Bari King as he stepped away from his chair.

"You can at least spare some more of your time and have some drinks with me later," offered Chief Domre.

"Chief I'm not much of a drinker, perhaps when I get what I want, we'll sit down and have this drink," stated Bari King, as he turned away from Chief Domre.

"There's no harm in being hopeful, but remember that my daughter will offer you something that is more than hope," articulated Chief Domre as he gazed at Bari King's retreating figure.

The sandy dirt road bounded by an array of mud houses with thatched roofs, created an impoverished ambience that brought a depressing quality upon Bari King's mood. His men followed his example, as he quickened his footsteps in a bid to escape from the stifling poverty that engulfed the village.

Evening's light bestrode the atmosphere as Bari King sat up on the bed. His desire to visit the famed beaches of the village got the better part of him, as he stood up leisurely from the bed. Parting the curtains, he peered through the sliding aluminium window. Picking up the local wrapper on the bed, he reinforced his wish for some privacy and aloneness. With the wrapper firmly secured about his waist, he picked up a white singlet. In the living room, the sight of Bari King's unusual attire drew muffled laughter from Jumbo. Smiling playfully back at him, Bari King positioned a face cap on his head and advanced towards the door.

"I'm going to the beach," stated Bari King.

"Alone Boss?" voiced Jumbo with a note of concern.

"Yes! Alone; I'll be okay," replied Bari King, reaching out for the door knob.

On the streets, Bari King blended in with the locals. Feeling the pistol, tucked away inside his jeans shorts, he felt reassured. He adjusted his wrapper and focused ahead.

The exuberant waves of the Atlantic Ocean enchanted him, and the sandy beach was hospitable to the soles of his feet. The rhythmic roaring of the ocean and the sight of coconut trees swaying gently in the wind inspired soothing feelings within him. As the vibrant waves spilled onto the sandy beaches, he leisurely caressed its foamy residue with his right feet. A relaxed smile, caressing his face, nurtured the energy that directed his gaze into the distant reaches of the ocean. He was thankful for the sparse population of natives that milled about the beach. The sight of a young woman suddenly animated his memory. He turned briskly towards her direction again and realized with a fresh wash of mild excitement that it was Kasi, Agila's daughter. He appraised Kasi for some fleeting seconds and then decided to approach her. Walking leisurely towards her, he wondered about the outcome of the looming encounter with her.

"Kasi, how are you this evening?" voiced Bari King as he gazed genially at her.

"Good evening sir," replied kasi, straightening her well proportioned petite frame and gently straining her head to catch a better glimpse of Bari King's face,

"Sir it's hard to recognize you in our local attire," continued Kasi, cradling an open calabash that was filled with colourful shells.

"I'm glad you recognized me," expressed Bari King, removing his face cap and putting it back on his head, after a few seconds intervened, "your shells are beautiful," continued Bari King.

"Thank you Sir," responded Kasi

"Bari will do; call me Bari," stated Bari King, glad that no other person was within earshot.

Kasi's courteous smile did not harbor any encouraging marker.

"You were particularly kind with your gestures, during my visit to your home; and I want to show some appreciation," articulated Bari King, reaching into the pocket of his jeans shorts and retrieving some naira currency notes, "please accept this token," continued Bari King, extending the notes towards her.

"I did nothing special Sir, the money is not necessary," posited Kasi.

"Take it any way," persisted Bari King calmly.

"No sir; thank you; I have to get back home," stated Kasi as she hurried away from Bari King.

Believing in Kasi's unassuming nature and lack of lust for money, Bari King gazed at her retreating outline. His encounter with her triggered an unrelenting longing inside Bari King's soul. He yearned for a woman with her kind of unworldly attributes. He was convinced that a woman like her would greatly inspire him to transform his current boisterous lifestyle. He thought about his girlfriend, Nengi, far away in Lagos, and acknowledged her striking physical endowments. In his reckoning, her other attributes were less than remarkable. Moved at the deepest core of his being, he continued to focus on images of Kasi and the loving promises that attended to them. Although Kasi's outline had completely disappeared, he continued to gaze in her direction, with eyes tinted by a wistful glint. Turning towards the ocean, he adjusted his face- cap and dug his right feet into the sandy beach. Reluctantly, he turned his back on the ocean and its beach and headed back to their quarters.

To welcome the brand new morning, Bari King stretched languorously on the bed. He alighted from it and advanced towards the bathroom. Relaxing on the sofa that adorned the living room, after breakfast, Bari King closed his eyes.

"Boss, there's a lady at the gate," announced Jumbo as he halted beside Bari King.

"A lady?" voiced Bari King as he puckered his face.

"Her name is Yena," continued Jumbo.

"Yena.... Yena..... Yena, okay I remember now; let her in," uttered Bari King as he sat up.

Gazing at the threshold of the living room, he hoped that Chief Domre sent her daughter to him with some good news.

Yena waltzed into the living room and gestured her tall and dark frame provocatively before Bari King. Her tight-fitting jean trousers highlighted her full figure. She flaunted a boldness bestowed by her alluring feminine attributes.

"Hello," greeted Yena, as she flashed an uninhibited smile.

"How are you?" responded Bari King with a courteous smile

"Fine," replied Yena.

"Sit down," beckoned Bari King, as he pointed to a sofa diagonal to himself.

"Thank you," stated Yena, sitting down.

94

"So what news do you bring from your father?" inquired Bari King calmly.

"I brought myself; is there a better package than myself," blurted Yena coquettishly.

"How do you mean?" asked Bari King, feigning ignorance.

"I came to keep you company, if I must blurt it out," continued Yena, still maintaining eye contact with Bari King.

"Thank you for your thoughtfulness, but I'm..... doing okay by myself," expressed Bari King politely.

"You can do better with me by your side, isn't that obvious," voiced Yena patiently.

"Look! You're a beautiful woman, but I have plenty on my mind; maybe if times were different, we could have hit it off," patronized Bari King tactfully.

"I'm beautiful but not good enough for you," averred Yena with a wistful smile.

"No! No! No! Don't say that, it's just that I have plenty of distractions now, and I won't be of much use to you," stated Bari King.

"Then allow me to be your refuge from all the cares and troubles of the world," volunteered Yena.

"Please! Please! Please! Yena it is?" uttered Bari King, raising his eyebrows- a gesture requesting for confirmation from Yena.

Nodding in the affirmative, Yena displayed a slight tinge of sadness in her eyes.

"I have many enemies who are dying to destroy me, and plotting my downfall is a major preoccupation of the Government; as you can see, I don't have much future to offer you," continued Bari King.

"Do you really want me to go?" asked Yena with a weak smile.

"Wait a moment," requested Bari King, rising up and advancing towards the bedroom. Retrieving some currency notes, he appeared in the living room once more.

"Please take this as a token of my goodwill," stated Bari King, extending the money to her.

"Thank you," voiced Yena appreciatively, collecting the money and standing up. Her smile flaunted a stubborn quality that pricked Bari King's suspicions. As she turned away from him, he wondered if the encounter would be their last.

Evening's light brooded over Bari King as he lay on the bed. He thought about Kasi and wondered if she would be at the beach. Rising up from the bed with bright hopes, he reached out for the local wrapper. He adorned it about his waist and covered his upper body with a plain white t-shirt. He promenaded out of the premises and headed towards the beach. His disguise worked well on the streets. The sight of the vibrant blue ocean spiked up his energy level. Barefooted, he gently stomped about the sandy beach with eyes that betrayed his mounting enthusiasm and enjoyment. He glanced about the beach with prying eyes in search of Kasi. With an air of disappointment, he folded his hands behind his back. He leaned against a coconut tree and gazed into the endless horizon that over lighted the ocean. He ignored the sprinkling of natives that populated the beach and immersed his attention in the hypnotic roaring of the ocean. He ignored the streams of vocalized conversation from two young men, standing behind him. However, the mere mention of the name, Kasi, jarred his attention and drew it away from the ocean. Steadying himself, he focused downwards at the sandy beach and sharpened his attention in a bid to gleam more information from the boys.

"Kasi was with me this afternoon," vaunted one of the boys.

"You are dreaming indeed," responded his companion.

"Dreaming? I'll show you something that'll convince you very soon," continued the young man.

"You don't have anything," persisted his friend.

"Don't underestimate me; I'm not even afraid of his father even if he is the greatest medicine man in this village," declared the young man.

A blast of irksome feelings swept across Bari King's soul as he realized that the subject of their conversation was the same Kasi that animated the longing of his heart.

"So what do you have?" queried his friend.

"If you follow me home and help me to repair my fishing net, I'll tell you everything and show you everything," proposed the young man with a sportive grin.

"Alright! Come on let's go," blurted his friend in a tone that sought to hold him accountable to his word.

As they sauntered away, their giggling aggravated Bari King's disappointment. Plagued by vexing feelings, he glanced at the blue ocean and failed to rediscover its enchanting quality. He relieved the coconut tree of his weight and focused towards their quarters.

The morning promenaded along the usual path allotted to it by nature. The austere ambience of Chief Domre's palace failed to uplift Bari King's mood.

"So what do you have for me?" began Bari King, as he sat opposite Chief Domre.

"I've not made any headway with Agila; I told you that he's a stubborn man," blurted Chief Domre.

"So where does that leave us?" asked Bari King in a level voice.

"I don't know where you stand now; there is the option connected with my daughter; it may be the only way for now," declared Chief Domre with an elfish smile,

"Chief, if I may restate again, that option is not on the cards," voiced Bari King calmly.

"Well! Suit yourself, I can't imagine what you have to loose by marrying my daughter," uttered Chief Domre, as he threw both hands in the air with mild exasperation.

"Chief, there must be another way, and I'm counting on you to find it," articulated Bari King in a determined tone.

"Look! I'm not a magician," declared Chief Domre.

"There is plenty of money to be had; don't forget that," whispered Bari King in a conspiratorial tone, as he leaned towards him. Smiling playfully, Bari King rose up from his chair, "Chief I'll be seeing you soon; you better have something for me, if you don't want the money to fly away through the window," continued Bari King with a sportive grin.

With airs near desperation, Chief Domre gazed at Bari King and swallowed hard. He racked his brain, as he gaped at Bari King's retreating outline.

It was the turn of evening's light to illuminate Bari King's bedroom. He stood by the window and pensively gazed outwards. He thought about Kasi and wondered if the damning stories from the strange youths were true. His longing to see her again filled him with hopes that he found difficult to unravel. Suppressing doubts about her virtue, he donned his usual native attire and promenaded away from the bungalow.

Stepping on the sandy beach, he welcomed the vigorous ocean wind. He gazed into the limitless blue expanse of the ocean and marveled at nature's grandeur. Reluctantly veering away from the ocean, he surveyed the beach. Unexpectedly, his roving eyes suddenly fell upon a scene created by Kasi and Yena, and he widened his eyes with a start. Suspecting that the scene would be lacking in friendly gestures, he hurried towards them.

As the distance that separated him from them narrowed, he beheld Yena, shaking her finger menacingly at Kasi and storming away. Offering no word to Yena, Kasi maintained a composed countenance.

"What was it all about?" voiced Bari King, as he stood few seconds away from Kasi.

"You should know better than me," retorted Kasi calmly.

"I'm in the dark here," asserted Bari King.

"Get your friend to shine some light for you," continued Kasi, betraying no emotion.

"Which friend are you referring to?" asked Bari King with a mild tone of impatience.

"The one that just left here; she came here to threaten me because she believes that I'm a threat to her ambition to be your wife," revealed Kasi as she shook her head incredulously.

"I don't believe it," blurted Bari King in a halting tone.

"You better do; maybe you need to run along and comfort her; she was quite worked up, when she left here," stated Kasi, as she smiled in a self-reassuring manner.

"There's no need for that; there's nothing between us," voiced Bari King firmly.

"Well! I wish you well in your stay in our village," stated Kasi calmly.

"Kasi, you forgot your purse in my room," came the voice of a young man, from behind them.

"Who are you? And what are you talking about?" queried Kasi, arresting her motions and turning backwards. Her glowering eyes wandered from the man's countenance to the red leather purse, in the man's outstretched arm.

"Don't act as if you don't know me again, after all we have done together," continued the man as he sheepishly lowered his arm.

"I don't even know why I'm wasting my time with you," retorted Kasi as she turned away from the stranger, "ehh.....heh! I know who sent you; tell Yena that she's wasting her time with me," blurted Kasi, with a knowing smile, as she turned sharply towards the stranger again.

Peering closely at the man, with an enlarging glint of suspicion, Bari King recognized him as the man that was gossiping with his friend about Kasi. It was just yesterday, and he remembered the man very well.

Lunging at the man with lightening speed, Bari King held him by the throat and steadily applied pressure.

"Who sent you here?" barked Bari King menacingly.

"Please don't hurt me," whimpered the man with a terror-stricken countenance.

"Answer me now before I crush you throat," threatened Bari King, ignoring the alarming expression that seized Kasi's countenance.

"Please don't hurt him; they don't really pose any threat to me; besides, there's no need for you to stress yourself over me," voiced Kasi with a note of concern as she gaped anxiously at them.

People, scattered about the beach and at varying distances from them, began to point curiously at them.

"Yena sent me; she planned it all," blurted the stranger as he gasped desperately for air.

As Bari King released his grip on the man's throat, his former victim instantly bolted away. Turning briskly backwards, Bari King beheld Kasi in the distance. She promenaded homewards with a clear focus. Withdrawing his eyes from her disappearing outline, Bari King gazed pensively at the blue expanse of the ocean and closed his eyes; uncertain feelings crept into his mind.

Pounding towards their quarters with reluctant footsteps, Bari

King acknowledged the sadness in his heart and was unsure of its origin.

Reclining on a sofa in the living room, Bari King welcomed the mellow light of the morning.

"Boss! There is bad news," began Jumbo as he halted beside Bari King.

"What kind?" asked Bari King, abruptly sitting up on the sofa with alert eyes.

"Imani has gone rogue with the men under him, they are reported to be raping and extorting the villagers within their vicinity," stated Jumbo.

"You're very sure about this situation?" voiced Bari King as he stood up.

"I wouldn't come to you with patchy news," uttered Jumbo.

"Why would he sign his death sentence?" articulated Bari King, as he gestured incredulously with both hands.

"I've already sent someone to infiltrate the village and gather intelligence," stated Jumbo.

"Good! Good! Is the person back?" queried Bari King pensively.

"Yes Boss," replied Jumbo.

"We are going to ride hard on him and his gang in two days time; get the men and our weapons ready," ordered Bari King in a determined tone.

"Boss there's another thing. We suspect that he's trying to align himself with Power Donga," revealed Jumbo calmly.

"I see!" ejaculated Bari King, nodding his head pensively, "we ride in two days time," blurted Bari King, jerking his head bolt upright.

Turning away from Jumbo, he advanced towards the bedroom. He donned a pair of black jeans and a white t-shirt and then faced the door. His mind trained on Chief Domre's palace, he briskly walked out of their quarters.

Adjusting the pistol under his white t-shirt, he strode into Chief Domre's palace.

"Chief how's your day going?" voiced Bari King with a genial smile as he sat opposite him, without waiting for an invitation.

"You've seen me and our village," retorted Chief Domre with an air of indifference.

"Chief something has come up; you should be able to use this situation to convince Agila to provide me and my men with his protective medicine; some of my men have gone rogue in a neighbouring village; they are pillaging and raping; your village is at risk now; I want to go over there and stamp out the menace; I'll be doing your people some good by doing that; there are enough reasons for Agila to respond positively to me now," stated Bari King in a lively tone.

"Umm! Does it mean that you're loosing control of your men," posited Chief Domre with a wry smile.

"Let's not digress here and get into side talks," blurted Bari King in an icy tone, staring at Chief Domre with unflinching eyelids, "shortly, you'll hear how hard my justice descends on those who run foul of it," he added.

Nervously, Chief Domre adjusted his faded white singlet, littered with pin-holes, and briskly veered his eyes away from Bari King.

"I suggest you go ahead; I'll meet up with you at Agila's place," managed Chief Domre in a steady voice.

"Okay!" replied Bari King in a steely voice, rising up from his chair.

His thoughts filled with optimism; Bari King marched past the gates of Chief Domre's palace and headed straight to Agila's compound. He paid scant attention to the poverty ridden and weather-beaten streets.

"So what can I do for you today?" began Agila in a genial tone, as he gazed at Bari King.

"You know what I want," replied Bari King calmly, sitting opposite him, inside his compound.

"Kasi, bring the native gin," beckoned Agila, slightly raising his voice and mildly straining his neck towards the main building, "that is what I can offer you now," continued Agila, turning towards Bari King and broadening his smile.

"I'm certain that you can offer me more than that," voiced Bari King with earnest conviction.

"I'm just a village herbalist, nothing more," posited Agila.

"There is danger at your gates; some miscreants in a neighbouring village are raping and pillaging; I want to go over and stamp out the madness before it gets to your village; that will be doing your village a big favour; the least you could do for me and my men is to support us with your protective rituals and medicine," stated Bari King in an unwavering tone.

Positioning a roughly-hewn table between them, Agila smiled and shook his head incredulously.

"I have to give it to you; your persistence is something not ordinary," voiced Agila with an accommodating smile.

"Does it mean that we are getting somewhere together?" asked Bari King, as his face lit up with hope.

"I have not changed; I'm still a village herbalist, nothing more, nothing less; if you are suffering from any ailment, I'll be glad to help; I can only offer help not power," replied Agila calmly.

The sound emitted by a door as it swung on its hinges distracted Bari King; and he turned towards its direction. He sought to initiate eye contact with Kasi, whose hands were well-laden with an enamel tray, but she tactfully evaded him. Reluctantly veering away from Kasi, Bari King focused briefly at Agila and then turned his attention towards space.

"Good afternoon sir," greeted Kasi, without batting an eyelid towards Bari King's direction.

"I believe it's still morning; good morning to you," reciprocated Bari King with a pleasant smile.

Setting down the well-worn enamel tray, littered with dark patches, on the wooden table between Agila and Bari King, she smiled courteously. After repositioning the bottle of locally-brewed gin and two glasses on the tray, she briskly walked away.

"Why do you always wear a friendly smile? Is it that you don't have any worldly cares at all," asked Bari King, with a curious glint about his eyes.

"I have peace and contentment," voiced Agila calmly.

"How can you be contented in this village, where you are surrounded by poverty and lack?" continued Bari King.

"We live in two different worlds," voiced Agila in a relaxed tone.

"And you obviously prefer yours to mine," stated Bari King with a knowing look.

"I'm okay," replied Agila.

"We're no longer strangers to each other; the least you could do for me now is to show me a little more kindness," continued Bari King with a smile.

"I haven't been exactly cruel to you, have I?" countered Agila in a mild tone.

"Why are you refusing us the rituals of the protective medicine," queried Bari King curiously.

"I've told you more than once that I'm just a village herbalist," averred Agila calmly.

Smiling and focusing an unwavering gaze at Agila, Bari King stood up. His expressions betraying his disbelieving notions, he turned away from Agila. Pounding on the dirt village road with firm footsteps, he sought to banish every iota of fear in his heart and reassure himself.

Sailing away from the village that harboured them for the past few weeks, Bari King looked back at the familiar sights of the village with a wistful glint in his eyes. He thought about Kasi and wondered if their paths would ever cross again. He sailed in the company of ten other log boats. They were dressed like ordinary village fishermen and blended well with the locals on the waters. An assortment of automatic and semi-automatic weapons, and military combat uniforms covered with black tarpaulin fabric and camouflaging netting usurped the position of fishes on the boat.

In the lead boat and under the cover of raffia palms, Jumbo cautiously waved them to stop. They quickly retrieved all their weapons and military-styled camouflage uniforms and disembarked from the boat. Still utilizing the shade of the raffia palms, they stood on the banks of the river and quickly attired themselves in their camouflage uniforms. With shoulders hung with magazines of bullets, automatic and semi-automatic weapons, they readied themselves for action.

"Boss! We are very close to Imani's camp," whispered Jumbo, as he turned towards Bari King.

Bari King nodded in acknowledgement and focused ahead. With murderous intentions, he cradled his fully automatic Uzi machine gun.

"They don't have any sentry on this side of the river," continued Jumbo.

"We have the element of surprise; we will form a semicircle about their camp and crush them without mercy," voiced Bari King confidently, as he appraised his men.

His men nodded vigorously in support of his statement. They

began to fan out as they advanced towards Imani's camp. Cautiously, they used their machetes to cut through the thick shrubs that confronted them. Boisterous voices of men cut through the forest and prompted Bari King and his men to become more guarded with their footsteps. They sighted a clearing in the forest populated by a band of men reveling with bottles of locally brewed gin and palm wine. Their weapons were scattered about them, and their few sober comrades heedlessly slung their weapons about their shoulders. Bari King and his men ignored the thick canvass tents that dotted the clearing and focused their attention on the self-indulgent men. They crouched on all fours and stealthily advanced towards the unsuspecting men in a semi-circular formation.

Imani, forcefully dragging a teenage girl towards his tent, suddenly came into their view. His jeering smile mocked at the girls protestations.

"Nothing should happen to the girl," commanded Bari King with quiet authority.

With a single wave of his hand, his men sprang upwards with lightening speed and opened fire on Imani and his men.

7

Surprised and shaken by the lightening attack of Bari King and his men, Imani and his comrade's response were feeble, compared to the ferocity of their attackers. Anguished cries of falling men rent the atmosphere and conspired against the natural harmony of the forest. His carnal pursuits long forgotten, Imani made to escape from the clearing but was trapped down by Bari King's men. When the sound of gunfire finally died down, Bari King and his men dominated the forest clearing, littered with blood and guts. Acknowledging with pride that there was no fatality on his side, Bari King advanced menacingly towards the cowering Im,ani.

"Boss, please forgive me; it was the devil that tempted and led me astray," pleaded Imani in a desperate tone.

"I hope the girl is safe," blurted Bari King as he turned backwards.

"Yes Boss! She's okay," replied one of his men.

"Devil eeeh!" voiced Bari King derisively, as he turned towards Imani, who was surrounded by Bari King's men, with their weapons pointing at his head, "you're about to take a trip to meet with this devil, who is now your master," stated Bari King ominously.

"Boss I beg you, if you spare my life, I will dedicate it completely to you," entreated Imani with tears running profusely down his cheeks.

"You are worthless to me; I don't have any need for you," expressed Bari King, as his men created space for him.

Unmoved by Imani's desperate pleas, Bari King pointed his assault rifle at him. With a cold and expressionless countenance, he drew a bloody line along Imani's leg with his weapon. Imani's cries failed to attract any sympathetic glance or attention within the forest clearing.

"Boss! please!" cried Imani with a contorted expression.

"How does that feel?" barked Bari King sternly, "reserve your pleas for the devil when you get to hell," continued Bari King, as he triggered a fatal hail of bullets.

"Let's get out of here," commanded Bari King, turning towards his men.

Cautiously, they trooped down to the river bank and donned their local attires. They secreted their assault rifles and camouflage uniforms in the belly of the boats and headed homewards.

The sound of the outboard engine was the only sound they welcomed as they sped onwards.

Disembarking on the familiar banks of the river, near their camp, they retrieved their weapons and camouflage gears. Shrill cries of insects, in the near-by forest, eloquently praised the unyielding presence of dusk.

Bantering boisterously with their comrades, the leading group entered their camp. Reverent nods were directed towards Bari King's direction as he made his way into the camp.

"Jumbo!" snapped Bari King, as he sat in front of his tent.

"Yes Boss," replied Jumbo, hurrying towards him.

"Go and get Mr. Gerard," commanded Bari King.

"Right away Boss," responded Jumbo, turning away from him.

Bari King surveyed their well-illuminated camp and nodded his head with satisfaction.

A sportive grin adorned his face as he beheld Mr. Gerard.

"I can see that you're adapting well," began Bari King, expanding his mischievous grin.

Mr. Gerard stood before him, unsure of how to respond to him

"You're clean shaven and appear more relaxed and better poised; you're quite a sight to behold; so what's the secret?" mocked Bari King.

Mr. Gerard wringed his hands nervously and darted his eyes to and fro uncontrollably.

"How's the toilet washing business? How does it compare with your former job?" voiced Bari King, roaring with laughter and getting up from his chair.

Rooted at a sport, Mr. Gerard twitched the features of his face nervously. Turning for the last time towards Mr. Gerard, Bari King chuckled with devilry under his breath and entered his tent.

Symphonic singing of birds announced the arrival of a brand new morning.

Bari King stretched before his tent and focused towards Mr. Gerard's tent. As he strode onwards, he acknowledged the greetings of his men with vigorous shaking of his clenched right fist.

"Come out!" barked Bari King as he stood in front of Mr. Gerard's tent.

Rushing out instantly with jerky motions and bare shoulders hung with a t-shirt, Mr. Gerard began to adjust the leather belt about his waist and don on the t-shirt.

"Come on! I want to see how good you are with toilet washing," blurted Bari King, roaring with an impish laughter.

In the background, his comrades cheered with the zest of men waiting for an entertaining spectacle.

Without hesitation, Mr. Gerard ambled towards the parade of

toilet units. A roguish grin animated the features of Bari King's face as he followed him. Mr. Gerard stopped before a toilet unit and entered it. Through the door that was left wide ajar, Bari King peered inside the toilet and cackled with laughter. The sight of Mr. Gerard, in the motions of cleaning the toilet continued to feed his impish expressions.

"Not a bad job Frenchman," blurted Bari King after some minutes, "you're not doing badly in your new vocation," continued Bari King, nursing his face with an air of satisfaction.

His deep concentration on his task sought to safeguard his consciousness from Bari King's intruding presence.

"Sonu! What can you make of your Boss?" asked Bari King, turning towards Sonu, who was standing beside him with an elated grin.

Sonu turned towards Bari King and enlivened his wicked grin.

"Who's the Boss now?" bellowed Sonu with a mocking grin, drawing closer to the door of the toilet.

Mr. Gerard turned sharply towards Sonu and quickly withdrew his attention. The feverish motions of his hands mirrored his rising terror.

The bright rays of noon failed to pacify the dis-satisfied expression on Akoju's face. He sat opposite Bari King and did not make any attempt to hide his discontent.

"So why are you tying to engage another medicine man? Haven't I served you with total devotion," began Akoju solemnly.

"Who told you that?" voiced Bari King with an impish grin, staring at a bottle of locally brewed gin that stood between them.

"Nothing remains hidden forever," asserted Akoju calmly.

"Anyway! There's nothing to it; I just want to reinforce what I have," stated Bari King.

"What you have does not need any reinforcement; I'm the

best medicine man around," vaunted Akoju, as he gently leaned towards Bari King for emphasis.

"Still, there's no harm in being ambitious," replied Bari King as he invigorated his grin.

"That ambition is uncalled for," uttered Akoju with vehemence, "look at you, you are hale and hearty; no bullet has pierced your body, and it is all thanks to my medicine," declared Akoju.

"Maybe I'm good at what I do," replied Bari King, chuckling under his breath.

"Don't be too sure about that; my medicine has served you too well," posited Akoju, as he reclined on his chair.

Grinning and shaking his head playfully, Bari King glanced backwards at his tent and poured some of the gin into Akoju's glass.

Sedate atmosphere of the evening surreptitiously crept upon Bari King's camp. Morale was quite boosted in the camp and they were in high spirits. All manner of automatic and semi-automatic guns together with magazines of bullet hung about their shoulders. All sorts of grenade and rocket launchers were also evident. All of them were equipped with military-styled camouflage uniforms and night vision goggles. The camp was teeming with hundreds of eager men. A sea of black berets bobbed to and fro.

As Bari King, bedecked like his own men, stepped out of his tent, they cheered wildly with clenched fists, vibrating vigorously in mid-air.

With a single wave of his hand, silence reigned in the camp. Flanked by his lieutenants, Bari King proudly appraised his men.

"Today we are going to strike mercilessly at Power Donga and his men and tell them that we are the true masters of the jungle. The sky and earth, on which we are standing now, will bear witness to this fact today. Listen attentively to the breeze; it is already praising us with victorious melodies. Every stamp of our feet will emit mournful beats, heralding the destruction of our enemies. Be courageous and remember all we rehearsed. We encircle them and attack from all directions," voiced Bari King vigorously. A calmness, aware of its ephemeral nature, suddenly set upon the camp.

"Show no mercy," bellowed Bari King.

"Yeah!" chorused his men, as their vigorous fists invaded the atmosphere oncemore.

Bari King beckoned on Akoju, standing few seconds away from him, with his hand.

Mindful of the reverent stares directed at him by the assembled men, Akoju advanced towards Bari King with metrical steps. He held a bottle that contained a plain coloured concoction. The sight of a live snake wriggling inside the bottle enhanced the solemnity of the moment.

"The rites are done; remember to tell your men not to touch anything that doesn't belong to them. The ones that will fall today are those not strong enough to keep to the commands and dictates of my medicine. Take a swig and pass it round to your men; everybody must drink from this bottle," concluded Akoju solemnly, as he held the bottle towards Bari King.

Taking the bottle from him, Bari King tasted the concoction. The blank expression on his face failed to betray any emotion. He handed the bottle to a lieutenant by his right. Akoju dutifully monitored the bottle as it passed from one man to another and refilled it at certain intervals.

The charged atmosphere within the camp triggered a queasy sensation within Mr. Gerard. His entire frame was overcome by tepid perspiration. He felt like relieving his bowels but was afraid of venturing outside.

"We are set to ride, and we will ride and strike as hard as hell," roared Bari King, swinging his head to and fro with a fiery glint about his eyes.

"Yeah!" chorused his men in a robust tone

They separated into four groups and went towards the river bank. They boarded waiting launches and sped off. After gliding on the river for about forty-five minutes, they beached the boats and disembarked. With nimble motions, they hid the boats in the nearby bushes and readied their weapons. On foot, they advanced for another ten kilometers in the forest, before Power Donga's camp loomed before them. Instantly, they broke into four formations and began to encircle the camp in the camouflage of darkness. Their night-vision goggles were their mainstay and they were in crouched positions. The men with the grenade launchers were at the forefront. Bursts of grenade fire suddenly rent the atmosphere and destroyed the machinegun nests, strategically positioned at certain points on the perimeter of Power Donga's camp. It was a signal that propelled Bari King and his men into action. With lightening agility, they sprang forward with ferocious eruptions of their automatic assault rifles. The unexpected attack caused utter pandemonium inside Power Donga's camp. Agonized cries of men tormented the atmosphere and sabotaged courageous voices, urging fellow comrades to fight back and throw off the invaders. Blood and innards created bizarre landscapes in the camp. Some of Power Donga's men were cut down as they made to escape from their besieged camp. Their counterattack, feeble and uncoordinated, was no match for the ferocity of Bari King and his men. The surprise and lightening attack tore at the morale of the defenders. More agonizing cries from Power Donga's men assaulted the sanctity of the surrounding forest and disturbed the natural order of the forest. Birds and other animals scurried away in terror.

"I want Power Donga for myself; capture him alive," yelled Bari King, straining his voice above the din of battle.

As his men overcame the last pocket of resistance, Bari King briskly scanned the confines of Power Donga's camp.

"Where is Power Donga?" barked Bari King with a nasty frown, ignoring the cries of the wounded, lying on the ground.

"Boss I have him," shouted Jumbo, emerging with a cowering Power Donga.

Power Donga was visibly shaking and his head was hung down.

"Move!" growled Jumbo, as he viciously prodded him with the butt of his rifle.

He sauntered towards Bari King with unsure motions. His limp and bloodied shorts and white shirt highlighted his pitiable image. His lethargic arms and downcast countenance only fueled a vindictive drive within Bari King. Lifting his head timorously, Power Donga made to survey the carnage and destruction that was wrought upon his camp.

"Look at me!" barked Bari King in a nasty tone, interrupting Power Donga's mournful and mental reverie. Fearfully contorting the features of his face, he cast a nervous look at Bari King and hung down his head again.

"Who's the king of the jungle now?" vaunted Bari King as he swaggered menacingly towards Power Donga.

With the butt of his assault rifle, he swung viciously at Power Donga's kneecap. Staggering and twisting his face in pain, Power Donga managed to maintain his balance.

"Huh! So your legs do not know what is best for you," snarled Bari King, as he delivered a savage kick, with his right boot, against Power Donga's knees.

Terrorized by Bari King's haughty grin, Power Donga buckled under his knees. A desperate expression hugged the features of his face, as he glanced upwards at Bari King with entreating eyes.

"Where are your tough words now?" mocked Bari King with a distasteful expression.

The shock of the surprise attack was still with the loser, and he nodded his head, up and down, in a woebegone manner.

"Look at me now!" barked Bari King, standing above him with a threatening pose.

With a lethargy sponsored by fear, he turned towards Bari King.

"You are looking at the true and only King of the jungle, and his image will be the last thing you'll see before you take a trip to hell," snapped Bari King as he instigated a rain of bullets from his assault rifle. The bullets froze the terror-stricken expression on Power Donga's face and left him in a bloody heap. Reassured by his deadly attack, Bari King turned away from Power Donga's remains.

"How many of our men are down?" asked Bari King, facing Jumbo.

"Five dead and eight wounded," replied Jumbo.

"Get our men together, we're riding out," directed Bari King.

"Some of Power Donga's men are lying on the ground, wounded," reported Jumbo.

"Let them live to tell the story, move them away from the camp and set everything on fire," commanded Bari King.

With unmitigated vigilance, Jumbo clutched his assault rifle and proceeded away from Bari King.

With their dead and wounded, they proceeded away from the burning wreckage of Power Donga's camp. The night sounds resumed their usual routine, as they made the trip back to their camouflaged boats and launch. As Bari King glanced upwards at the full moon, his concern about his future dulled his sense of victory.

They retrieved their boats and began preparation for the return trip back to their camp. As they sped off into the night, the calm waters yielded completely to them.

An air of celebration overtook their camp as they entered. They took their wounded to the sick bay, manned by a qualified medical doctor and some male nurses. They took their dead to another section, where some attendants were waiting to receive them.

"Jumbo!" called Bari King, as he towards Jumbo's direction. He stood few inches away from his tent and waited for Jumbo to come within earshot.

"Get out a message to our men, and make sure that they promptly
compensate the families of our fallen comrades," averred Bari King.

"Right away Boss!" replied Jumbo, slightly bowing respectfully and hurrying away.

Entering his tent, Bari King stretched out on his bed. His shoulders were still hung with his assault rifle as he closed his eyes. Sleep was very far from his eyes. Images of his comfortable home flitted to and fro in his mind. He yearned for the long lost ease of lounging about in his home.

The morning waved a new banner of freshness. Alert, Bari King stood in front of his tent and appraised the various motions that populated his camp. Suddenly veering towards Mr. Gerard's tent, he leisurely sauntered towards it. Along the way, he responded to the greeting of his men, by slightly raising his right hand.

"Open this tent!" barked Bari King impatiently. Sound of awkward motions from the tent filtered into his ears.

Mr. Gerard's motions were uncoordinated as he unzipped his

tent. He staggered out of his tent and managed to maintain his balance. His face was mildly contorted and he slightly swayed from side to side. His white t-shirt and blue pajamas were disheveled in a manner that brought more impairment upon his charm.

"What the hell is wrong with you?" asked Bari King in an unsympathetic tone.

"I'm not well at all; I am feeling very weak and feverish; I hardly slept last night," stated Mr. Gerard in a shaky voice. His shivering frame entertained countless goose bumps.

"I'm not here to be entertained by your whining, and for your information– I'm not your nurse,"voiced Bari King sternly.

"I'm really not well," continued Mr. Gerard.

"Who cares!" lashed-out Bari King.

"I really need some medical attention," entreated Mr. Gerard.

"You better remove yourself and your grandmotherly wailing from my sight, and go to the sick bay," intoned Bari King with his facial features creased by disgust.

"But I...... don't know where the sick bay is," blurted Mr. Gerard, fidgeting uncontrollably.

"Wait for me to materialize a miracle that would lead you to the sick bay," ejaculated Bari King, eying Mr. Gerard scornfully and turning away from him.

"And let me tell you one thing; you are next on my agenda, stated Bari King, as he made a sudden turn, "don't think that you can use this phony sickness of yours to evade me," continued Bari King with unabated hostility.

Staring at Bari King's retreating outline, Mr. Gerard shuddered and applied all his strength to steady himself. With trepidation, he composed himself and began to survey the camp. With a mind plagued by confusion, he tottered back into his tent. Collapsing on his bed, he stared blankly at the side of the tent.

Rising up weakly from his tent, Mr. Gerard prepared himself for his morning bath. He retrieved the towel and soap provided for him and weaved his way towards the bathroom.

Mildly refreshed by his morning bath, Mr. Gerard lay on his bed and contemplated on his next move. Rising up, he braced himself and strolled towards the door. Standing outside his tent, he scoped-out the camp. Uneasy feelings still antagonized his innards as he advanced towards a man. He felt slightly relieved by the kind visage, he believed the man possessed.

"Please can you direct me to the sick bay," began Mr. Gerard weakly, hoping for the best.

The man turned towards him and impersonally appraised him from head to toe.

"The last tent by the left," replied the man without betraying any emotion.

"Thank you very much," voiced Mr. Gerard with genuine gratitude. The unexpected show of civility and kindness boosted his energy level slightly.

He sauntered towards the sick bay and aligned himself to routes that were sparsely populated by Bari King's men. With timid motions further highlighted by the high temperature of his body, he walked into the sick bay. Unsure of himself, he stood inside the tent and viewed the large expanse of space. By his right and close to the door, a male attendant sat behind a table and regarded him noncommittally. There were rows of beds on both sides and some of them were occupied by patients, who bore wounds on different parts of their body. Cautiously, he ambulated towards the attendant.

"How may we help you sir?" began the attendant courteously, gazing at him calmly.

"I need some medical attention; I'm not feeling well at all," complained Mr. Gerard, slightly emboldened by the attendant's politeness. He hoped that his mannerliness was not part of some ploy that would eventually lead to an undesirable ending for him.

"Please sit down," continued the attendant, pointing to a chair in front of his table.

Mr. Gerard obliged him and occupied the chair; the attendant then pulled out a drawer from the table and retrieved some equipment. He got up from his chair and fetched a file from a standing steel cabinet. After checking Mr. Gerard's vital signs and weight, he commented inside the file and closed it.

"What is your name sir?" asked the attendant.

"Gerard Henri," he replied.

"The doctor will see you now," voiced the attendant, after writing against the file.

Mr. Gerard trailed after the attendant, who focused on one of the cubicles at the other end of the tent. The doctor calmly chucked aside the book he was reading, when they entered his cubicle.

"Please sit down," addressed the doctor politely, gazing calmly at Mr. Gerard.

As Mr. Gerard sat down in front of the doctor, the attendant placed his file on the doctor's desk and left.

As the doctor read through the file, Mr. Gerard assessed him to be in his mid-thirties. His natty attire of blue jeans and white t-shirt also caught Mr. Gerard's attention.

"So how exactly do you feel?" continued the doctor, lifting up his head.

"I have general body weakness, I felt feverish all through the night, though the fever has somewhat subsided, and my appetite is not good," stated Mr. Gerard with a strained countenance.

"Please lie down on that examination table," directed the doctor gently, pointing towards his right. He then retrieved a pair of latex gloves from a packet lying on a side table. He ambulated towards Mr. Gerard's prostrate form and began to examine his stomach.

"Are you feeling any pain or discomfort?" queried the doctor.

"No.... Not at all," replied Mr. Gerard.

"Okay, you can get up now," stated the doctor, as he removed the latex gloves and dumped them inside a refuse bin, "you are exhibiting the classic symptoms of malaria and we need to treat it aggressively," continued the doctor as he sat down behind his desk and began to write inside Mr. Gerard's file.

"Take the file to the nurse out there, he knows what to do," dictated the doctor, handing the file to Mr. Gerard.

"Please do something more for me; help me!" whispered Mr. Gerard in a desperate and entreating tone.

"If you are talking about helping you to escape, that one is beyond me, there's nothing I can do about that; I can only help you to get better," replied the doctor sympathetically.

"You seem like a nice person; why are you running with this kind of bunch?" queried Mr. Gerard curiously.

"Crude oil spillage and gas flaring from the operations of the company you work for degrade our environment and cause health problems for my people, some have even died as a result of this unfavourable situation; why are you involved with the oil company?" posited the doctor with a smug expression.

"But a lot of the oil spillages are direct results of vandalisation of pipelines," stated Mr. Gerard, eager to reason with the doctor.

"We are done here; take your file and leave," blurted the doctor curtly, stiffening the features of his face slightly.

"Sorry," ejaculated Mr. Gerard, rising abruptly from the chair and hurrying out of the cubicle with his file. The doctor's abrupt tone roused him from his forgetfulness, and the sad emotions prompted by his predicament assailed him once more.

He sauntered towards the male nurse and handed the file to him.

"Please sit down," directed the male nurse politely, opening the file, "have you eaten?" continued the nurse.

"No," replied Mr. Gerard.

"A battery of injections is prescribed here; you need to go and eat," counseled the nurse.

"I'll go now and find something to eat," stated Mr. Gerard, rising up from the chair and glancing at his watch.

In a bid to avoid the hostile looks of the wounded men, who occupied some of the beds in the tent, he kept a straight face as he walked out.

Avoiding paths clustered by Bari King's men, he made his way to the dining pavilion. His heart sank as soon he sighted Bari King inside it. He dutifully cued up and waited for his turn. Without looking towards Bari King's direction, Mr. Gerard felt Bari King's gaze intensely focused upon himself. His stomach rumbled as it acknowledged his uneasiness. He did not dare to shift his gaze for fear of making eye contact with Bari King.

"Frenchman, you're going to man the pots this morning, so go behind the table," blurted Bari King, roaring with laughter.

A chorus of supporting laughter from his men reverberated within the dining pavilion and further darkened Mr. Gerard's dread. Hesitating, Mr. Gerard toyed with the idea of using his enfeebled circumstance as an excuse.

"Get behind that table now," barked Bari King menacingly, taking some vigorous steps towards Mr. Gerard.

With shaky motions, Mr. Gerard hurried towards the table

laden with an assortment of food items. Wearing a sportive grin, the man who was stationed behind the table untied his white apron and extended it towards Mr. Gerard. With unsure motions, he reached out for it and began to tie it about himself. Befuddled, Mr. Gerard stared at the steaming food and their gleaming stainless steel receptacle. Rising tempo of raucous cheers from the assembled men tugged at Mr. Gerard's attention and he lifted his head. His poise continued to suffer as he beheld Bari King approaching him.

"Let me have jollof rice and fish," stated Bari King, as he stood before Mr. Gerard.

With unsteady hands, Mr. Gerard dished out some food, according to Bari King's request.

Bearing an impish smile, Bari King collected the food from him and ambled towards a steel post. Leaning against it and munching his food, he eyed Mr. Gerard intermittently.

"Take your own food and get out of that spot," ordered Bari King with a slight edge to his voice, after Mr. Gerard had served three of his men.

Grateful and relieved, Mr. Gerard took some stewed fish and hurried away from the table.

The afternoon sky beamed cheerfully at Bari King as he sat in front of his tent. Turning leisurely towards his right, his entire frame suddenly recoiled in utter alarm.

8

With features begging for reassurance, he stood up abruptly from his chair and peered into the narrowing distance.

Loosely hanging his white t-shirt about his shoulders and still staring into the distance, he began to shake his head incredulously. Bari King steadied himself and waited for the three figures approaching him.

"Oroma! What are you doing here?" blurted Bari King, unable to suppress his alarm as he gazed at his sister.

"I'm happy to see you alive and well," voiced Oroma as she beamed at him.

"This is no place for a woman," chided Bari King gently, trying to reason with her, "Why did you bring her to this place," queried Bari King, turning towards his men and raising his tone sharply.

"Boss, she wouldn't let go, and she threatened to come here on her own, if we don't take her along," articulated one of the men, with a desperate expression that sought to sell the rightness of his actions to Bari King.

"So! what now?" posited Bari King, softening his tone and turning towards his sister.

"I've seen you alive; the first part of my mission is fulfilled," stated Oroma calmly.

"Mission?" ejaculated Bari King. His countenance readied him to absorb more surprises from his sister.

"Take her bag to the second tent," commanded Bari King,

glancing at the man with the bag.

"Yes Boss," replied the man, dutifully maneuvering her bag towards the tent.

"Let's go inside," suggested Bari King, pointing towards the second tent.

He led the way, and Oroma followed closely behind. The tent was quite spacious and comfortably furnished. The mattress, table-top refrigerator and reading table ably mimicked the convenience of a home. She sat down on the mattress and turned towards Bari King, who was pulling out a chair.

"Mama and papa are really worried," began Oroma ruefully

Bari King's head was hung-down and he was boxed in by doleful emotions elicited by his sister's words.

"I'm sure you've heard about the amnesty program of President Yar'adua; this is a very good opportunity for you to move away from all the violence and make a new beginning," continued Oroma in an earnest tone that invited hope to drive her melancholy away.

"I've heard about it, but I don't know how sincere the Government is," expressed Bari King, shrugging his shoulders skeptically.

"Bari, I think the Government is quite sincere and serious," countered Oroma in a mild and convincing tone.

"How do you know that?" queried Bari King, still nursing an unbelieving smile.

"Many militants in the Niger-Delta area are already surrendering and coming under the umbrella of the amnesty programme; and so far, they are not voicing any regrets," averred Oroma.

"It is still too early to run into conclusions," stated Bari King.

"Bari, the program is real, I know you're smart enough to know that," enthused Oroma. Her candour sought to chase her brother's skepticism away.

"We'll see how it goes," replied Bari King.

"Don't give me that political statement," voiced Oroma with a smile.

"Since when did I become a politician," reciprocated Bari King with a genial smile.

"I won't leave here without a yes from you, that is the only word our parents are waiting to hear," said Oroma with a determined look.

"Don't start on that stubborn line," chided Bari King with playful gestures of his head.

"I mean what I said," asserted Oroma with a determined expression.

"How are Mama and Papa?" enquired Bari King, as he struggled to reign in emotions threatening to overwhelm his bravado.

"They will be better when you leave this jungle," revealed Oroma.

"What of Nengi?" voiced Bari King with a knowing smile.

"I can't say much about her; I don't follow her about; however, between you and your money, I don't know the one she loves more," posited Oroma.

"Okay! Let's go somewhere else; when are you leaving this camp? It's no place for a woman," stated Bari King calmly.

"You already know my answer to that question," the determined look in her eyes bravely challenged Bari King.

"Hmm!" exclaimed Bari King with a questioning look in his eyes, "have you eaten?" he continued.

"I'm okay," she replied.

"I'll give you time to rest," stated Bari King, rising from the chair.

"I didn't come here to rest; I came here to get you home." Her unwavering tone sought to etch the essence of her visit deep within her brother's mind.

"Just rest; we'll talk later," coaxed Bari King.

Few seconds away from the door of her tent, Bari King turned and flashed her a kindly smile. As he continued his advance to his own tent, he was gladdened by his sister's genuine love and concern for him.

Benevolent rays of morning's light enveloped Bari King and his sister. They were both peering unto the distance, at the uninspiring sight presented by Mr. Gerard. Mr. Gerard, donning a pair of blue jeans and white t-shirt, staggered from side to side. The amusing laughter of the nearby men greeted the spectacle and filtered into their ears.

"Is that not the Frenchman?" asked Oroma with a note of concern and eyes still glued on Mr. Gerard.

"Yes!" replied Bari King.

"What is wrong with him?" continued Oroma.

"He complained of feeling unwell yesterday; I believe he's receiving medical attention," stated Bari King, unmoved by Mr. Gerard's condition.

As Mr. Gerard lost his balance and fell to the ground, Oroma sprang towards him.

"Oroma!" voiced Bari King with a rising pitch, leaning abruptly towards her direction.

Oroma ignored his deterring call and continued to head towards Mr. Gerard, who was still panting heavily on the ground.

"Come on, I'll help you back to your tent," addressed Oroma sympathetically, as she leaned towards him.

A hush descended on the onlookers and they quickly melted away. They were unsure of Bari King's reaction and did not want to be at the receiving end of any fallout.

Mr. Gerard regarded her with a suspicious look and did not budge from his position.

"Its okay," reassured Oroma.

With a resigned expression, Mr. Gerard staggered to his feet. He weaved sideways as he gazed at Oroma. Reaching out towards him, Oroma took his right arm and placed it against her shoulders.

"We can walk gently back," stated Oroma, smiling warmly at him.

Apprehensive about how the next scene would unfold, Mr. Gerard took the first step. His awareness of Bari King watching from a distance made him to become more self-conscious. He made concerted efforts not to lean heavily on Oroma. Mr. Gerard's limbs intermittently quivered nervously, as he wondered about the relationship between the kind lady who supported him and Bari King.

"Thank you very much for your kindness," volunteered Mr. Gerard, stepping away from Oroma, when they were few seconds away from his tent.

"It's Okay," replied Oroma in a perfunctory manner, turning away from him, "were you going to get some food?" asked Oroma, abruptly veering backwards.

"Yes!" confessed Mr. Gerard.

"So what would you like to eat; I'll help you bring it," proposed Oroma.

Mr. Gerard hesitated and wondered about the wisdom of assenting to her request.

"It's okay; you can tell me," coaxed Oroma in a benevolent tone.

"I usually take white rice and fish pepper soup," stated Mr. Gerard.

"Done!" voiced Oroma, veering away from him.

Sauntering towards the door of his tent, Mr. Gerard sensed the ugly forms of suspicious thoughts deep within his mind. He wondered about the authenticity of the unexpected kindness that was coming his way.

Leaning against a guava tree beside his tent, Bari King gazed at his sister with a countenance that betrayed nothing.

With metrical steps, Oroma advanced towards the dining pavilion. The assembled men hastily made way for her and she arranged Mr. Gerard's breakfast in a tray. With the well-laden tray, she promenaded back to Mr. Gerard's tent. The line of Bari King's sight trailed after her as she continued on her mission.

"Your food is here," announced Oroma, in front of Mr. Gerard's tent.

"Thank you very much for your kindness; I don't know how to repay you for this," articulated Mr. Gerard in a voice laden with gratitude, as he appeared through the door of his tent.

"Don't worry; it's all in a day's work," voiced Oroma with a cheerful smile.

Managing a weak smile, he nodded appreciatively and received the well-laden tray. He walked to the table inside his tent and gently placed the tray on it.

Sitting on a chair, Mr. Gerard wondered about the unexpected turn of events surrounding him and yearned for his good fortune to outlast any misfortune or ill will lurking in the shadows. Burgeoning feelings of accomplished vitality accompanied him, as he reached out for his food.

Whistling lightheartedly, Oroma advanced towards her tent. An amusing smile played on the features of Bari King's face as he observed Oroma.

"What do you think you're doing," queried Bari King, when she came within earshot.

"Bari how do you mean?" replied Oroma gently.

"You know exactly what I mean," countered Bari King calmly, still spotting an amusing smile.

"I'm just spreading some love in your camp," declared Oroma with a spirited smile.

"Heee! You're out of place here; there's no place for bleeding hearts in this camp," voiced Bari King in a calm and unwavering tone.

"Bari, he has a family like us, and they must be worried about him," stated Oroma in a sober tone.

"Who cares about that?" retorted Bari King.

"Bari you are a kind and loving man at the core of your being; I'm your sister and I know you very well; all these militant postures are just masks destined to fall away; I've come here to remind you of who you are," postured Oroma with a determined expression.

With a clement look about in his eyes, Bari King gazed at his sister and then set his eyes into the distance. The gyrating green leaves of the surrounding trees failed to entrance him. Emotions welled-up within him and eroded his vitality.

She gazed kindly at her brother and offered sympathetic feelings that could not be captured with words. She turned away and pensively walked back to her lower tent.

Bari Kings eye's trailed after her. Deep within him, he was gladdened by her arrival. Her knack for making trying and pressing situations seem surmountable endeared her to him. He deeply treasured her lighthearted ways.

Mellow light of morning claimed its turn in nature's roaster. Oroma briskly advanced towards Mr. Gerard, who has just emerged from his tent with a bunch of clothes. He paused in his tracks, when he beheld Oroma. A warm smile readily reciprocated by Oroma played on his face.

"Good morning," greeted Mr. Gerard

"Good morning to you too, and how are you feeling today?" replied Oroma in a genial tone.

"I'm much better today," continued Mr. Gerard.

"Are you planning to do some laundry?" queried Oroma with a note of concern.

"Yes," replied Mr. Gerard.

"But you are in no condition to do any laundry," stated Oroma, as she shook her head emphatically.

"Please I don't mean to be rude; to me you are an angel in shining halo that has come to lift my burdens and sorrows away; but still, I can't resist the urge to ask who you are," articulated Mr. Gerard calmly, displaying the mantle of affecting emotions that was perceptible about his eyes.

"I'm Oroma; and I am Bari's sister," replied Oroma with untainted cheerfulness.

Mr. Gerard's face stiffened with dread, as Oroma's word rang in his ears, and his bunch of clothes fell to the ground.

"Yeah! Yeah! I know that you must convinced that Bari King is a vicious thug and monster; but truly deep inside, he is nothing like that," averred Oroma, as she stooped down and began to gather the spilled clothes, "Here you are," continued Oroma, offering the clothes to Mr. Gerard, who was still transfixed at a spot.

Hastily regaining his composure, he accepted the clothes.

"What you're doing; I don't think it will turn out right for me," stated Mr. Gerard as he blinked nervously.

"Oooh! Don't worry, I'll prove to you that Bari is not a monster," responded Oroma, almost chiding him.

"Are you sure about that? I could be in real serious trouble if he thinks am messing with you," voiced Mr. Gerard.

"I'll live up to my words; you'll see," stated Oroma in a lighthearted tone.

"By the way, you don't have to do any strenuous work," continued Oroma, reaching out and taking custody of the clothes, before Mr. Gerard could offer any resistance, "go back to your tent and rest; I'll take care of the clothes," directed Oroma firmly.

Lost for words, Mr. Gerard turned and ambled back to his tent. A maze of thoughts traversed his mind and imbued a pensive quality to his countenance. Fresh gusts of hope swept across his entire being and heightened his sense of wellbeing.

With a cheerful glint still dancing in her eyes, Oroma advanced towards the laundry bay.

"Please wash these cloths directed Oroma in a courteous tone, as she stood before one of Bari King's men, who was busy at the laundry bay.

"But they belong to the Frenchman," whined the man.

"He is not feeling well today, so I'm asking you to be of help," continued Oroma in a calm and unwavering tone.

Frowns littered the man's face and gave birth to reluctance inside his mind. He rinsed detergent lather off his hand and veered towards Bari King's tent. The sight of Bari King failed to greet him and he focused on the clothes that were been offered to him by Oroma. With heavy motions he reached out and collected the clothes from her.

"That is very nice of you; thank you very much," voiced Oroma gratefully. She turned and headed back to her tent.

The afternoon plodded on, along the predestined path, outlined for it by nature. She sat behind Bari King's tent with alert eyes. Straining her senses, she truly rebelled against the meaning in the snippets of conversation filtering into her ears; Bari King and Akoju were deeply enmeshed in a dialogue in front of the tent.

With clear contours of irritation evident on her face, she stood up.

"To strengthen you more and more, there's a ritual we need to perform," voiced Akoju, leaning towards Bari King, who was seated opposite him.

"I've participated in several rituals; is this one necessary? If it is money you want, just go ahead and ask," posited Bari King with a countenance that betrayed nothing.

"You know that I don't like it when you start on that path," resisted Akoju.

"Which path? Are you talking about the path of money? You and I know that you enjoy walking on that path," continued Bari King with a mischievous smile.

"It is not a secret that I like money, but that is not why I'm here; I'm here to protect your interest first," asserted Akoju

Walking urgently to the front of the tent, Oroma distracted Bari King and Akoju. The look of surprise on Akoju's face greeted her.

"Bari' I need to talk to you," began Oroma in an urgent tone, ignoring Akoju.

"Okay!" replied Bari King, standing up and searching her countenance.

Bari King followed her as she briskly walked towards the rear of the tent.

"Bari don't do it," stated Oroma in a self possessed tone, when some reasonable distance separated them from Akoju.

"Do what?" queried Bari King with a playful smile.

"Bari you know exactly what I mean; don't entangle yourself into any ritual again; remember you're getting out," articulated Oroma in an entreating manner.

Gazing at her sister, who in his estimation truly cared about him, sparked off a deep longing within him, which steadily supplanted his playful smile.

"Okay! We'll see," voiced Bari King in a tone that belied the countless thoughts that roamed his mind.

"Bari! Now is the time to get out of all this," her voice was firm, and the expression on her face still laboured to sell her counsel to him

Without uttering any more word and with robust footsteps, Bari King walked back to the front of his tent.

"Bari, your sister's presence in this camp is putting you at risk," stated Akoju. The tone of his voice had a dire prophetic ring to it.

"Shut up!" snarled Bari King, jumping angrily to his feet, "What do you know about my sister?" continued Bari King with blazing eyes.

"Bari, you need to be on your guard." Akoju's voice was tame and he did not dare to look Bari King in the eyes.

"It's time for you to go," barked Bari King, storming into his tent.

The sudden discord between Bari King and Akoju gladdened Oroma's heart. She considered it a good and positive omen. She resolved in her mind to relentlessly pursue her cause for the sake of his brother's welfare.

The light of the afternoon disseminated its warmth selflessly, unaware of the longing that seized Mr. Gerard's mind. Sitting on a log, under an Iroko tree, Mr. Gerard earnestly yearned to behold Oroma's kind countenance. He mentally acknowledged and appreciated the ease and most natural way with which she expressed her kindness. With his thoughts, he imagined different scenarios that had a heavy dose of Oroma's love and kindness in its background. A smile played on his face, insulating him from his current reality and predicament.

"Where do you think you are?" castigated Sonu, as he advanced towards Mr. Gerard, "you better wipe off that smile from your face before I darken your afternoon," he continued, showing obvious signs of irritation.

Still fired by the euphoria of his daydreaming, Mr. Gerard unflinchingly faced Sonu. A smile still caressed the features of his face and his lips were pursed defiantly.

"You are destined to be a loser," blurted Mr. Gerard.

"What! What did you just say," snarled Sonu, inching closer to him.

The ugly expression on Sonu's face prompted a suffocating sense of dread within Mr. Gerard. He cringed as the smile disappeared from his face.

"I know what your plan is; we are all seeing through it, hanging around the Boss' sister will not save you," continued Sonu with unabated belligerence.

Mr. Gerard faced away from him, and his chest heaved up and down, in a shallow rhythm.

"I thought you were brandishing your newfound courage," retorted Sonu with a crooked vaunting smile.

"Sonu, is there a problem?" interjected Oroma in a courteous tone, as she approached them from behind.

The sound of her voice startled Sonu; and he turned abruptly towards her.

"No! Not at all," blurted Sonu, as he managed to regain his composure. With uneasy motions, he wiped his face with his right hand and hastened away from the scene.

Colour returned to Mr. Gerard's face. A smile of gratitude, resting on the deep feelings that she inspired inside him and the sweet air of relief fanning across his soul, animated his face.

"How are you today?" inquired Oroma with a pleasant smile, as she inched closer to Mr. Gerard.

"I'm feeling much better now; beholding your beautiful face is doing the magic," declared Mr. Gerard, as he stood up.

"You're looking it," complimented Oroma with a pleasant smile.

"Is it really safe for me to be speaking with you?" queried Mr. Gerard in a tone, mildly compromised by worry.

"Bari is not a monster." Her smile was unblemished by Mr. Gerard's uneasiness, and her deep conviction in her words lifted the mild crease off Mr. Gerard's countenance.

"I'm glad you're on my side." He relished the sweet air of relief prompted by her words.

"Exercise more patience; everything will be alright," reassured Oroma.

"Goodness and kindness flow with so much ease from your heart." His eyes were still cloaked by poignant emotions inspired by her presence and reassurance. "It would be a great blessing to have you in my life," confessed Mr. Gerard with unrestrained and earnest airs.

"Can you boast of backing up your words with sincere actions?" Her eyes searched his countenance for evidence of his sincerity.

"Since my kidnapping ordeal started, I considered myself luckless and unfortunate; however, your coming has righted every ill suffered by my heart; your kind presence is inspiring an enrapturing tune within me." He fully displayed his countenance before her and earnestly hoped that she would catch more than a glimpse of the deep feelings she inspired within him.

"Are you sure of your words." The expression in her eyes buttressed her feelings.

"If only my feelings could talk for itself, it would sound more eloquent than me," declared Mr. Gerard.

"Don't flatter me because of your desperate desire for freedom."

Her expression still challenged him to prove his words.

"My feelings are beyond the realm of flattery." Deep feelings swirled within him and dictated the manner with which he blinked his eyes.

"My promise to help you is truly unconditional," averred Oroma.

"You see what I mean," blurted Mr. Gerard in an animated tone, "kindness and selflessness ooze from every fiber of your being, and that is part of the quality drawing me towards you," he continued with brightly lit eyes.

"You've just known me for a couple of weeks; is that enough for you to run into conclusions?" prodded Oroma.

"You touched me in a manner that defied time and space; the grind and toil of physical time cannot be associated with an ounce of the deep feelings that you inspire inside me," declared Mr. Gerard with renewed burst of energy.

"Your words sound nice, and the emotions cladding your eyes are quite touching, but I'm not yet convinced," stated Oroma, shaking her head to underscore her point.

"Eemm! What part are you not convinced about?" His words were drenched with his eagerness and attentiveness.

"You're a Frenchman, and we hear a lot about your kind," avouched Oroma.

"Please don't believe everything you hear; besides, the strength of the feelings you inspire inside me will never permit me to do something that is contrary to love," professed Mr. Gerard in an earnest tone

"So tell me how you plan to transcend the racial divide?" The curious glint in her eyes was clearly visible to him.

"It is just now that you're reminding me that our colours are different; the deep feelings that you inspire inside me has elevated me to a realm, where race and colour has thinned out," he expressed with a broadened smile.

"I've heard enough for one day; it's time for me to go," expressed Oroma with a genial smile.

She turned away from him and made to leave the secluded shade of the Iroko tree.

"Please wait," beckoned Mr. Gerard in an earnest tone," I just want to thank you for the minutes you spent with me' though few in physical estimation, they are inimitable pearls treasured greatly in my heart. Thank you for transporting me to another realm, where my physical shackles loose their potency," expressed Mr. Gerard in a tone reeking of emotions and gratitude.

Oroma smiled at him and then focused away. He was transfixed by a deep yearning in his heart as he stared at Oroma's disappearing outline.

Sitting alone, under the Iroko tree, he nurtured a dreamy and faraway look in his eyes. He replayed his joyful encounter with Oroma, in his mind, and reveled in the emotional fallout. He wondered at the strange coincidence, which started as a misfortune and eventually brought him into contact with Oroma.

He suddenly caught sight of Bari King and apprehensive thoughts stealthily crept upon him and sullied the effervescent colours of his emotions. He abruptly veered away from him and rose up. He focused at his tent and advanced briskly towards it.

The green foliage of towering trees gyrated mildly in gratitude to the soothing warmth of the morning.

Promenading briskly towards Bari King's tent, Sonu nurtured his thoughts with a determined expression

"Bari can I come in?" voiced Sonu, pausing in front of Bari King's tent.

"Sure! Come in," responded Bari King in a level tone.

"I hope I've not come at a bad time," began Sonu, in a manner that betrayed his preoccupied mind.

"It's okay; sit down," said Bari King, gesturing with a newspaper and waving him to a nearby chair.

I'm just here to report a situation that appears to be steadily getting out of hand; the Frenchman is forgetting his position in this camp," continued Sonu in a grave tone.

An intervening silence preyed mercilessly on Sonu's mind.

"What is your business with the Frenchman? You are the one, who has forgotten his place and position in this camp; keep away from the Frenchman; he is none of your business," chastised Bari King sternly, dropping his news paper angrily on the floor

"So........rry Boss!" stammered Sonu, scurrying out of the tent.

Oroma stirred on the bed inside her tent. Her pensive countenance mirrored the thoughts that were competing for a frontline position inside her mind. Pictures of Mr. Gerard's emotional confessions filled her thoughts. She was truly moved, almost to the point of being disarmed by his uninhibited ways with his emotions. The deep conviction blazing in his eyes and accompanying his words haunted her heart. A smile enlivened the features of her face, as her thoughts held on to a resolution.

Rising up from the bed with a zest bestowed by the birth of a new decision, she adjusted her jeans and white t-shirt. She promenaded out of her tent and focused towards Bari King's tent, lying beside her own. Bracing herself, she took a deep breath and became more conscious of her thoughts and emotions.

"Bari can I come in?" enquired Oroma.

"Sure, come in," accented Bari King, closing the newspaper in his hands and glancing towards the door of his tent.

She ambled into her brother's tent and sat opposite him.

"So what is eating at your mind?" probed Bari King with a

playful glint about his eyes.

"Well! How do I begin?" voiced Oroma with an expression that highlighted the conviction in her heart. A serious expression suddenly overcame the smile on Bari King's face and he leaned slightly towards her. "The Frenchman is showing serious interest in me," revealed Oroma in a tone that solicited for Bari King's understanding.

9

Instantly, the features of Bari King's face became flushed with anger and disapprobation. Rising abruptly, he mindlessly threw his book on the floor.

"What exactly do you mean?" queried Bari King, clearly exposing his disapproval. An incredulous expression made an appearance, now and then, on the features of his face.

"Bari don't act as if Henri is not a human being," voiced Oroma in an undaunted voice.

"Oooh! So you're now on first name basis with him," ejaculated Bari King, throwing both hands upwards in shock.

"Bari, I didn't ask for this to happen. I didn't come here to look for love; it just happened," stated Oroma in a poignant tone.

"What exactly are you telling me?" articulated Bari King, shaking his head and remonstrating with his hands, "are you telling me that you have fallen for the Frenchman?" continued Bari King.

"I wouldn't put it that way; he has made some confessions to me, and I want to take him up on his words," averred Oroma.

"What happened to all the young men flocking around you?" uttered Bari King, in a tone urging her to come back to her senses, "You don't even know anything about him," he continued.

"Bari, my eyes and senses are wide awake; you know that I am not easily carried away," stated Oroma.

"That is why I'm very fearful of this situation," he replied.

"You need not be," soothed Oroma.

"How?" blurted Bari King.

"Bari! What are you really worried about? Is it his European origins?" queried Oroma.

"I suspect that he might be manipulating you in order to gain his freedom," spilled Bari King; "by the way, what's the big deal about him," he added with a visible frown.

"There is this disarming openness about him that argues fervently in favour of his sincerity." The expression in her eyes betrayed her firm belief in her convictions.

"Please speak in a language I can understand," lamented Bari King.

"Bari, please don't take it this way; I truly appreciate the fact that you care about me and would always want to protect me," entreated Oroma.

"Romantic fiction is different from real life; don't allow yourself to be confused by ideas you pick up in fiction novels," he counseled.

"Bari, I am very much with my senses; I am not hopping into the next flight with him." Her reassuring expression was clearly visible to her brother.

"Well! I don't know what to expect anymore." The frowns that littered his face still revealed that the shock of her sister's revelations was still with him.

"How do you think mama and papa will react?" he continued.

"Leave that to me; I'll handle that at the right time," avouched Oroma confidently.

"Your courage and determination truly amaze me. Are you not worried that it may not work out? Both of you are coming from two different backgrounds," expressed Bari King, sitting down on a chair.

"Doubts creep up upon me sometimes, but I'm determined to give it a good try." Her dovelike expression tugged at her brother's emotions; and he mentally vowed to protect her no matter the circumstances.

* * *

The tranquilizing light of the evening was gradually establishing its dominance over the atmosphere.

Sitting on a log of wood near his tent, Mr. Gerard stared at the neighbouring forest. Thoughts of Oroma, the true captor of his attention, traversed all the nooks and crannies of his mind. A beatific expression on his face heralded more thoughts of Oroma. Memories of her beautiful face and loving kindness schemed together and spurned heady emotions deep within him. Completely immersed in his emotional reverie, he failed to notice Sonu as he approached him.

"You won't get away with it," blurted Sonu, in a nasty tone.

Turning towards him, Mr. Gerard bestowed a very genial smile upon him. Sonu's forbidding countenance failed to quench the light of his beatific feelings.

"I know what you are planning; you're planning to use Oroma as an escape ticket, but you're going to fail woefully; you are taking a big risk that will consume you," continued Sonu, with unabated belligerence, glaring hatefully at Mr. Gerard.

"That silly smile on your face will soon transform into tears of agony," snapped Sonu angrily.

Sonu's noxious stare failed to corrode Mr. Gerard's emotions, which continued to swirl in effervescent colors. Angrily; Sonu veered away from him and stormed off.

Amazed at the lack of ill-feelings within him, Mr. Gerard smiled and turned away from Sonu. He faced the surrounding forest and entertained images of Oroma's beautiful countenance in his mind. He experienced deeply rewarding feelings nurtured by the remembrance of Oroma's unique brand of selfless kindness.

He continued to enlist the help of thoughts centered on Oroma to transport him away from his world of captivity.

Nurturing a stern and forbidden expression, Bari King promenaded towards Mr. Gerard. Within Mr. Gerard's vicinity, he intentionally stepped on some dry twigs and distracted his attention. Mr. Gerard turned backwards abruptly. His smile died instantly on his face as soon as he beheld Bari King. He stood up abruptly and faced him. He cast furtive glances at him and sought to quell the rising fear threatening his innards. Mr. Gerard intentionally stood on the other side of the big log of wood and used it as a protective divide.

"I don't know what you're up to, but I want to tell you this, if you toy with my sister or her emotions, I will hunt you down wherever you are and destroy you; I want to assure you that I have the means and resources," stated Bari King in an inclement tone.

"I .... am not toying with your sister; her kindness is truly an inspiration to me," revealed Mr. Gerard in a voice rendered unsteady by his tremulous feelings.

"I don't care about your feelings; all I care about is my sister; I want to drive that into your consciousness," continued Bari King with a hard edge to his voice.

"I'm not a fool; I understand very well," replied Mr. Gerard meekly.

"Good for you," voiced Bari King, turning away from him.

Unsure of his next line of action, Mr. Gerard continued to stare at Bari King's departing outline. Sitting on the log of wood, he began to contemplate on Bari King's words. With a desperate longing evident on the features of his face, he imagined how the air of freedom would taste. As he continued to focus on Bari King's words, he felt the comforting feeling of hope.

* * *

The light of the morning witnessed countless thoughts vying for supremacy inside Bari King's mind. Deep in rumination, he sat on a chair inside his tent. With a countenance cradled by a deeply felt conviction, he rose from the chair. He walked out of his tent towards Oroma's tent. Pushing back opposing thoughts into the far reaches of his consciousness, he paused before Oroma's tent.

"Oroma can I come in?" voiced Bari King calmly.

"Sure! Come right in," replied Oroma unzipping the tent to peer out at her brother.

Smiling warmly at him, she stepped out of the way. He walked into her tent and sat down on a chair.

"I've given thought to a lot of things," began Bari King in a somber tone and preoccupied manner; "and I've reached some conclusions. Now is a wise moment to transform our armed struggle into a political one. To that end, I've decided to accept the amnesty offer," stated Bari Kind with a moderate smile of relief.

"Bari you've made me so glad today, oooh!" voiced Oroma in a very bright tone, rising up from her chair and throwing her arms around her brother.

"Eeeh! Your decision is indeed timely and wise," enthused Oroma, pulling away and gazing at her brother with a contented smile. A warm smile enlivened the features of Bari King's face and his hands still rested on his laps.

"Mr. Gerard will be freed tomorrow. I know you very well; and I know how you can be, when you are bent on something; Please be careful; I don't want to see you get hurt; anyway I'll be watching from a distance," revealed Bari King, rising from the chair.

"Heee! Bari that's wonderful news," commented Oroma, with buoyant feelings.

"You should get prepared also; you are leaving tomorrow," continued Bari King. "I'll leave you to break the news to him," he declared, broadening his smile.

"Hee! Heee! Heee!" exclaimed Oroma, throwing her hand from side to side in a delighted manner; "Bari, you won't regret your decision today; today is indeed a great milestone in your life; all forces of good and light must surely be applauding your decision, today," spilled Oroma thoughtfully.

"Ummh! I have to get going; I have a lot to do," said Bari King, veering away from his sister, with an unburdened countenance.

The morning's bestowals illuminated the beautiful image of Oroma and the rapturous feelings associated with it, deep inside Mr. Gerard's consciousness.

He sat on a log of wood beside his tent and gazed into the neighbouring forest. The symphonic call of birds and the rhythmic dance of green foliage belonging to towering trees encouraged his line of thoughts. Varied magnitude of smiles adorned the features of his face, as his mind continued to roll out images of Oroma.

The mild sound produced by the impact of Oroma's legs against brittle leaves drew Mr. Gerard's attention. As he turned towards her, the smile on his face attained a higher degree. Stepping over the log of wood, he took a few definitive steps towards her.

Nice to see you this morning; the radiance of your beautiful countenance is surely uplifting my entire energy level," began Mr. Gerard, unabashed.

"I'm glad you are up and running," replied Oroma, in a jocund manner.

"Well... its thanks to you," he said.

"What wont you give to leave this place?" continued Oroma jovially.

"I'm not sure I want to leave this place anymore. Since your advent into my life I no longer feel the fetters of my captivity; your loving kindness gave my heart a brand new song of love; your beautiful radiance has lifted a lot of dross and heaviness away from my soul; I now feel the lightness of a man who truly loves and cares about you," expressed Mr. Gerard in a tone laden with emotions.

"You'll be freed tomorrow!' exclaimed Oroma, broadening her smile.

Mr. Gerard was still hooked on the beatific feelings inspired by Oroma's presence, and the impact of her words failed to register on his gestures.

"Really!" blurted Mr. Gerard, slanting his head and squinting his eyes, as the enormity of Oroma's words finally penetrated his consciousness.

"Yes! You'll be free tomorrow," reiterated Oroma.

"Orooma that's great news," enthused Mr. Gerard, throwing both hands upwards.

"Its Oroma not Orooma," corrected Oroma with a smile. "Why are you so eager to go? You made me to believe that you would endure any situation, once I'm close to you; have you been lying to me?" voiced Oroma, still maintaining a jovial smile.

"My heart is always pronouncing your name in a language that is non-physical. I am so glad because freedom will give me a good background to grow and express my love for you," declared Mr. Gerrard.

"I'm truly waiting for you to reassure me that your feelings and touching expressions are not just an escape from boredom and captivity," spilled Oroma thoughtfully.

"Don't worry; you're destined to behold countless manifestations of my feelings," stated Mr. Gerrard soothingly, "please don't forget to give me your phone number," he added.

Smiling coquettishly, Oroma veered away from him.

As he gazed at her disappearing outline, he began to savour the sweet taste of freedom, which his imagination made very real to him. Sitting back on the log of wood, he began to replay his recent encounter with Oroma. His smiles proclaimed a rosy future for him and Oroma.

Lost in his emotional ruminations, he failed to notice Sound, as he surreptitiously advanced towards him from the rear.

"You must be feeling very lucky indeed," began Sonu in a loathsome tone.

Turning towards him, Mr. Gerard continued to display his unaffected smile.

"Good morning it is!" exclaimed Mr. Gerard in a genial tone.

"You will not leave his place unscathed, I wi...." blurted Sonu, his voice trailed off as his roving eyes engaged Bari King's line of sight. With terror clearly clouding his countenance, he made a detour with his head, away from Bari King's direction, and scampered off. His eyes cold and unfriendly, Bari King rooted himself at a spot and focused at Sonu.

"Sonu!" beckoned Bari King in a commanding tone, when he came within earshot.

"Bbb... ari," stammered Sonu, halting in his tracks and turning towards Bari King.

"Come here," barked Bari King in an acrid tone.

Evading his eyes apprehensively, Sonu sauntered towards him.

147

"Why are you still hanging around the Frenchman?" queried Bari King in a forbidden tone, "if I catch you around him again, your fate will be worse than that of a skinned man; keep away from him; he's family now," spilled Bari King.

Furiously nodding his hung-down head in accent, Sonu scurried away.

The solemn silence inside Bari King's tent rubbed-off on morning's light.

"Jumbo, please sit down," voiced Bari King calmly, pointing at an opposite chair.

Jumbo sat down and patiently waited for his Boss to spill the contents of his mind.

"A window is opening through the amnesty program; we should be wise enough to take advantage of it; it is time for us to move into the stage of our struggle," stated Bari King, resting his arms on the table and leaning towards Jumbo. A thoughtful glint roamed the corners of his eyes and buttressed his intentions.

"Boss, you're perfectly right," responded Jumbo in an elated tone.

"Get the men together; I want to address them now," directed Bari King.

"Right away Boss," stated Jumbo, rising with brisk motions.

Gazing at the outline of Jumbo's back, he truly treasured his loyalty and support. He stretched himself on the bed and began to collect his thoughts together.

"Boss the men are ready for you," informed Jumbo, straining his head in front of Bari King's tent.

"Okay! I'll be out in a minute," replied Bari King, rising from the bed. He donned a white t-shirt and tied the lace of his white canvass shoes. He positioned a black beret on his head and adjusted his white t-shirt. Taking the first step towards the door of his tent, he paused in his tracks and removed the black beret from his head. He gently cast it on the bed and gazed wistfully at it. Steeling himself, he proceeded out of the tent. New thoughts that buttressed his yearning for peace engendered feelings of relief within him.

Squinting his eyes outside his tent, he glanced upward and advanced briskly towards the muster point. The animated voices of his men suddenly died-down as his figure loomed before them. He stood before the assemblage of his men and nodded his head with satisfaction. He glanced sideways and then focused ahead.

"Emh! We are now at a turning point in our struggle. I want to thank every body here for your loyalty and support. We are going to embrace the amnesty program of the Federal Government and move from the jungle into the political arena. Wisdom dictates that, at this juncture. There's money for everybody to start something meaningful .I hear that they are building camps for ex-militants; I want to assure you that the camp is not for you or me. We would meld back into society and take good care of ourselves. Please allow your mind-set to conform to the tone of my words," His roving eyes gathered whatever comfort it could muster and heaped it upon the gathering of his sober men.

Thunderous cheers suddenly erupted in the crowd. Throwing firsts in mid-air, his men boisterously chanted his name. He smiled and began to nod his head in acknowledgement.

The morning reveled in its newness and offered its gratitude to nature with bold displays of its cheerful light.

Oroma, bright and gay, hurried towards Mr. Gerard's tent. Glancing upwards, she appreciated the cheerful sky and allowed it to enhance the lightness in her steps.

"Henri!" she called, as she stood in front of his tent.

"Coming," he replied, from the confines of his tent.

The urgency in his tone elicited smiles from her face.

"Oroma, how are you this morning?" voiced Mr. Gerard with a pleasant smile.

"You're still not getting my name right, but I'll give it to you-you're trying," stated Oroma with an impish grin.

Mr. Gerard shrugged his shoulders and lifted his eye lids playfully.

"I'm leaving this morning," disclosed Oroma calmly.

I've already memorized your cell phone number, and I'll call you soonest," declared Mr. Gerard, stepping closer to her.

"I see!" exclaimed Oroma, Nodding her head and smiling.

"Your beautiful smile and the stirring expression in your eyes holds so much promise of kindness and love; just being close to you evokes gusting emotions deep within my heart," declared Mr. Gerard, gazing intently at her with unblinking eyes. He hoped for her to snatch a preview, through the screen offered by his eyes, of the inspired feelings surging within his heart.

They gazed into each other's eyes and their non-verbal compliments formed a bridge that connected their hearts.

"I have to go," stated Oroma, after some fleeting moments. She smiled at him and made a detour.

Rooted at a spot, Mr. Gerard gazed at her departing outline and continued to savour the buoyant feelings still swirling within him.

At a distance, Bari King leaned against a tree and allowed his line of sight to move between his sister and Mr. Gerard. He shook his head and smiled with amazement.

When Oroma disappeared from his sight, Mr. Gerard turned and focused towards his tent. Bari King straightened his frame and adjusted his blue t-shirt. He zeroed in on Mr. Gerard's tent and advanced towards it.

"Frenchman!" bellowed Bari King, in front of Mr. Gerard's tent:

Urgent rustlings within the tent heralded Mr. Gerard's advent from it. He stood before Bari King with a heart pounding nervously, and made repeated efforts to calm and reassure himself.

"Get ready; you're leaving this afternoon," voiced Bari King.

"This afternoon!" exclaimed Mr. Gerard, engaging Bari King with a smile and look of wonder,

"Yes, this afternoon," restated Bari King calmly," my people will take you to Presidential Hotel, where you'll be handed over to your own people," he continued.

"Thank you very much," affirmed Mr. Gerard, clasping Bari King's hand; and thereafter, abruptly unclasping it apologetically.

"A new suit and accessories will be delivered to you; please get ready," added Bari King calmly, as he smiled at Mr. Gerard.

As he gazed at Bari King's retreating outline, he wondered about Bari King's sudden transformation. Walking back to his tent, it struck him that he had not eaten breakfast. He paused and then veered towards the food pavilion. On his way, he welcomed the calmer and civil gestures of Bari King's men. He observed that the aggressive air that hung over the camp seemed to have melted away.

Sitting down before his plate of white rice and fish pepper soup, he observed that the taunting expressions and smiles usually directed at him were missing on the faces of the neighboring men. Lifting a spoonful of soup, he gradually began to let in thoughts that proclaimed resurgence of his fortunes.

After breakfast, he proceeded back to his tent without any incident. Having entered his tent, his eyes fell on a pair of trousers, matching shirt, and jacket. They were well laid-out on the bed, and he suspected that they were of a very good quality, as he drew closer to the clothing items. He caressed them gently and nodded his head in appreciation. His eyes strayed to a pair of dark leather shoes lying on the floor, and he pursed his lips in satisfaction. He gently shifted the apparels to one side of his bed and stretched out. His mind wandered back to the day of his capture. He closed his eyes and marveled at the tenacity of his spirit in surviving all his experiences in the jungle. He folded his arms against his stomach, and its heaving motions ensnared his attention.

Mr. Gerard felt buoyant and relaxed, as he dressed up. He hung his jacked against the back of the chair and sat down. Knowledge of his imminent departure inspired elated feelings deep within him, and he began to observe the items in the tent with a strange light.

"It's time!" came a voice outside his tent.

He stood up and grabbed his jacket, as the reality of the situation sank into his consciousness; he glanced about the tent for one last time and smiled. He emerged from the tent and stood before a neatly dressed man. The man appraised him and smiled.

"I can see that you're ready; let's go," continued the man, still smiling.

He led the way and Mr. Gerard followed him. Mr. Gerard made eye contact with some nearby men, and their lack of animosity reassured him further.

After some minutes, his eyes chanced upon Sonu. The ugly scowl on Sonu's face was still no match for the elated feelings that swirled within Mr. Gerard, and he managed to maintain the smile on his face.

A third well-dressed man joined them, and the trio advanced

towards the nearby river bank. They stepped on the sandy banks of the river and boarded an executive white launch. The water receded behind them as they sped away. Glancing about and looking into the distance, Mr. Gerard spotted several log boats, piloted by villagers. The non-threatening quality displayed by the boats enhanced his good state of mind.

Mr. Gerard welcomed the sights presented by solid land and clambered onto the jetty, as soon as the driver killed the engine. He conformed to the alignment of the two men, and they all walked towards a waiting dark Toyota corolla sedan. One of the men, who had and authoritative manner, passed instructions with motions of his head, and the driver of the car stepped out. Without any delay, the man occupied the position behind the steering wheel. His comrade sat beside him, in the front passenger seat. Without any prompting from the men, Mr. Gerard opened the rear door and entered the vehicle.

The driver maintained manageable speed and navigated through the short expanse of a dirt and motor-able road. As they veered into a tarred road, the air-conditioned ambience of the car helped to nurture countless thoughts cheering his impending freedom. Glancing about with a smile on his face, he appreciated the civil activities that claimed the roadside. He welcomed them as new harbingers of his normality.

They finally entered refinery road and began to speed towards Eleme Junction. At a road block, manned by a combined team of police and army officers, they were waved to a stop. The driver calmly complied and brought down the glass of his door. With a suspicious glint about his eyes, the military officer peered into their vehicle.

"Is everything okay?" queried the officer, focusing at Mr. Gerard.

"Officer, we're good," replied Mr. Gerard calmly.

"You can go," voiced the officer, withdrawing with cautious motions and still appraising Mr. Gerard and his two companions. The officer stepped backwards and waved them forwards. Glancing backwards as they sped off, Mr. Gerard observed the stacks of sand bags and battle ready army officers and wondered if the amnesty program of the federal Government would eradicate such anomalies on the roads.

The familiar sights of Aba road moved him deeply, and he truly treasured the meaning of freedom.

"We are driving straight to Presidential Hotel; your people are waiting there," stated the man behind the wheels.

"I'm fine with that," replied Mr. Gerard calmly.

As they drove into Presidential Hotel, he glanced upwards at the cheerful sky and silently shouted the word "freedom" within his mind.

Stepping onto the paved forecourt of Presidential Hotel with racing heart-beats, he welcomed the mild afternoon breeze and felt the warm embrace of liberating thoughts. Still in the company of his two companions, he ambled into the comfortable ambience of the reception lobby. His face lit up with a smile as he beheld a group of men approaching him. They were of European and Africa descent.

"Henri, it's good to see you," voiced a white man in front of the group, in an elated tone.

"I'm sure glad to be free," replied Mr. Gerard, shrugging his shoulders.

"Yes, I know, hope they didn't harm you?" continued the man in a concerned tone, as he lightly rested his right palm on Mr. Gerard's shoulders, in a show of sympathy.

"No sir; I'm fine," stated Mr. Gerard.

"Well, that's good to know," affirmed the man.

The exhilarated expression on the faces of the congregated men underscored the uniqueness of the moment.

"I came with these......," blurted Mr. Gerard, turning around to search for his companions, but they had altogether disappeared, "Ummh! I guess they have gone," pronounced Mr. Gerard, turning towards the man.

"Henri! Let's go; we need to get you to the clinic," averred the man with a mild note of urgency.

Mr. Gerard nodded in the affirmative, and they all begant o troop out of the lobby. As they advanced towards a waiting vehicle, he glanced upwards at the cheerful sky and was glad for the moments he was spending outside the confines of the jungle camp.

"Henri, you look different; there's something about the look in your eyes; well, I guess after such an experience as yours, one will not remain the same again," expressed the man, without turning towards him.

Mr. Gerard smiled and refocused ahead. As he entered the vehicle, he felt the walls erected about his mind by his self-preservation instinct as they crumbled away.

The cheerful morning sky beamed down at Bari King, as he sat in front of his tent. With good ease, he observed the transformed setting of his camp. The cheerful chirping of birds seemed to applaud the calm and relaxed disposition of his men. His contented expression heightened his inner conviction. He earnestly believed that he had aligned himself with the wise and right path.

Bari King puckered his face curiously as the image of Akoju loomed before him. He gathered the resources of his mind together and waited for him. With an unperturbed expression,

Bari King focused away from Akoju, as he drew closer to him.

"I've heard!" exclaimed Akoju in a ponderous tone, sitting beside Bari King, without waiting for an invitation.

"What exactly did you hear?" queried Bari King in a level tone.

"The amnesty of course," replied Akoju in a petulant tone.

"What about the amnesty?" voiced Bari King firmly?

"Bari, how can you ask me that? Have you forgotten the covenant you made with us; don't tell me that you have forgotten so soon about the protection we offered you; well, I just came remind you that the covenant is a lifetime one; there's no option for you to turn your back on us; you will continue to make money available to me, for the continuation of all the necessary sacrifices and rituals," expressed Akoju coldly.

"I'm done with that way of life; I'm moving into the next phase of my life, and I don't need your rituals anymore," asserted Bari King.

"You are very wrong there; if you turn your back on this covenant, there will be dire consequences for you to face," threatened Akoju in an ominous tone, as he stood up from the chair.

"Are you threatening me? You know I don't take kindly to threats," stated Bari King, rising up from his chair and flashing a disapproving smile.

"I'm sure you know quite well that you're not just dealing with me; there are supernatural forces and beings at play; think about that seriously," blurted Akoju with a lewd smile.

"It's time for you to be on your way; I'm through with you," voiced Bari King in an unflinching tone.

"We are not through by a long shot; you will see," retorted Akoju, still nurturing a crooked smile.

Gazing at Akoju's disappearing outline, he attempted to sort out his feelings. He made concerted efforts to dispel hints of anxiety that sought to penetrate his mind.

He sat down on his chair and began to welcome thoughts that would transform into harbingers of joy.

The afternoon flaunted its exuberant rays and enfolded Bari King and Jumbo. The background provided by their jungle encampment still endured.

"The crew that is coming to dismantle this place, I hope they will still arrive tomorrow?" began Bari King in a relaxed tone.

"Sure Boss, they'll be here tomorrow, "replied Jumbo.

"Okay!" exclaimed Bari King, nodding with satisfaction.

The mills of nature still active, it rolled out another brand new morning.

Bari King leaned against a Banyan tree and observed the busy men, who were dismantling the structures in his camp. A reflective expression played against the features of his face, and he pondered about the new phase of life that was inevitable for him. He gazed at the majority of his men, who still milled about the camp, and deepened his ruminative expression.

Mild midday sun enlivened the atmosphere.

Wearing a poignant expression, and with a handful of his men, Bari King gazed about his camp, shorn of any manmade structure. He shrugged his shoulders and veered towards the banks of the river.

"Let's go," commanded Bari King firmly, allowing his men to move ahead of him.

Few minutes away from the camp, Bari King turned backwards to catch one last look at his former camp.

"It's finally over," he muttered with relief deep inside his mind, as he focused towards the river bank.

They stepped onto the sharp sand of the river bed and boarded three white executive launches. When they got to a particular section of the river that usually inspired great sense of ease and safety within Bari King, he smiled and nodded his head. After a smooth ride on the river, they anchored and stepped onto the jetty. They were greeted by their comrades, who were within the vicinity of the jetty. Together they moved towards a larger group. Two Toyota Coaster buses, one Nissan mini-van, and four Toyota Corolla sedans were all lined up before them. Bari King entered the first sedan in the row and his men distributed themselves within the other sedans and buses. The Nissan bus had only one passenger in front while piles of different types of assault rifles, grenade launchers, magazines of bullet, and other armaments were piled up in its rear. The two Toyota buses led the way and the convoy sped away.

They were waved to a stop by a policeman, at a road-block manned by police and military personnel. Complying with the directive of the officers, Bari King lowered the rear side glass. A policeman cautiously approached and peered at him.

"Comedown," commanded the police-man rudely

"That's not necessary," replied Bari King in a firm and unwavering tone

"What do you mean by that?" barked the policeman, leaning menacingly towards him.

10

A tensed atmosphere separated Bari King and the policeman.

Another police officer briskly walked up to the vehicle and looked inside it. Gently coaxing his combative comrade away from the vehicle with his hands, he whispered some words into his ears and calmed his colleague with gently waves of his hand.

"So who cares if you're Bari King?" blurted the combative officer, breaking away from the mediating officer and taking a few steps towards Bari King.

Bari King regarded him with a contemptuous smile and lifted up the glass.

With little hesitation, they waved them forward, and they continued with their journey.

Without any other incident; they drove into Aba road and maneuvered into Stadium Road. They were briefly delayed at the main gate of the Liberation Stadium, the venue of the demobilization exercise, before they were let inside by security officers. They were directed to a parking area by plain clothed security personnel. Parking their vehicle, they alighted from them.

Sir, what of your weapons?" began a policeman, facing Bari King.

"They are all in the van," replied Bari King courteously, pointing at it.

"You need to get your men to move the weapons towards that

place," stated the policeman calmly, pointing in the opposite direction.

"You heard the policeman; move the van," voiced Bari King calmly, looking at the driver of the van. The driver duly entered the van and drove it with its contents towards the direction pointed out by the policeman.

"You also need to go and register with your men; the officers at that canopy will direct you accordingly," continued the policeman, pointing at a canopy situated within the main bowl of the stadium.

"Okay! Thank you," affirmed Bari King, smiling courteously at the policeman.

As he trooped out with his men towards the canopy, boisterous chants from other militant groups rent the atmosphere. They hailed Bari King with choruses of his name, and he responded by punching his right fist three times in mid-air.

Within the vicinity of the canopy, plain-clothed and uniformed security personnel arranged caches of weapons surrendered by the repentant militants. Piles of AK-47 assault rifles, grenade launchers, magazines of bullet and other armaments dotted the landscape. They presented a heart-numbing picture that was capable of troubling any rational mind.

"Please put your name here, your men will append their own after yours," directed a plain-clothed security officer, sitting under the canopy.

Bari King duly complied and stepped aside for his men to follow suit.

"The Federal Government has provided living quarters for ex-militants," informed the officer.

"No! That's not necessary for us; you have our data; if the need arises, you can always get in touch," asserted Bari King firmly.

160

"Just give me a minute," replied the officer, stepping away and conferring with a group of his superiors seated under another canopy behind them.

"It's okay, you can go, but we'll definitely be in touch," expressed the officer, occupying his chair once more.

"As you wish," stated Bari King, shrugging his shoulders and smiling.

As they advanced towards their vehicles, Bari King acknowledged the looks of admiration directed at him by other ex-militants. He glanced about the stadium and smiled, as he sensed the tensed atmosphere that overshadowed the demobilization exercise. He broadened his smile as he spied, through the corners of his eyes, some security officers stealing furtive glances at him.

Having reclined on the rear seat of the Toyota Corolla sedan, he longed for some peaceful time and rest. When they entered Stadium Road, their convoy dispersed in different directions. Bari King's vehicle was directed towards his newly acquired detached house, situated within GRA Phase I. The familiar sights of Port Harcourt evoked distant happy memories within him and he prevailed on his mind to milk them for all the goodness he could get from them.

He stepped onto the paved forecourt of his modest five-bedroom detached house and bade his comrades' goodbye. Walking up to the main entrance door, he welcomed feelings of ease. Before he reached it, it opened and revealed Nengi's womanly outline.

"Bari, it's good to see you again," voiced Nengi as she warmly embraced Bari King at threshold.

"I'm glad to be home," voiced Bari King, wrapping his hands affectionately around her.

They affectionately linked their hands together and walked into the living room.

"I'm really happy to have you back; now, I'll have the opportunity to show you how much I care about you," declared Nengi, smiling and flaunting her figure provocatively before Bari King. She removed her petticoat and hung it in the wardrobe.

"I'm hungry; can you get me something to eat," expressed Bari King, sitting down on the bed and letting out a lazy yawn.

"I've ordered for some food, and it will soon arrive," replied Nengi, moving her high spirits into a new gear.

"You can't even provide me with a homemade meal after all these moments of separation, and you say you want to show me how much you care about me," remarked Bari King, exhibiting a disappointed expression and shaking his head despondently

"Bari, don't talk like that; your conclusions are not fair at all; after all, food is food," blurted Nengi in a mildly irritated voice, standing at akimbo before Bari King.

"Food is food?" retorted Bari King, glaring at Nengi with a questioning look in his eyes.

"Bari, you just came back; let's not celebrate your homecoming with a fight," soothed Nengi, sitting down beside him and reaching out to wrap her arms around him.

Gently, he pulled away from her and stood up with fatigued motions. Turning his back on her, he began to remove his shirt.

"Do you at all care about the things that I like? You know that I cherish home cooking,; and still, you find it so easy to make those remarks," continued Bari King in a downhearted tone, still backing Nengi and busying himself with the removal of his clothes.

"If I don't care about you; I wouldn't have waited all this while for you," voiced Nengi, drawing closer to him.

"We'll see about that," remarked Bari King in a lightless tone.

"We'll see about that? What kind of statement is that? Are you now doubting me?" expressed Nengi in a doleful tone.

"I merely observed a situation that unfolded before me," replied Bari King, secreting his used clothes inside a laundry bin.

"Bari, you're tired; just take your bath and come to bed," counseled Nengi in a comforting tone.

Without offering further words, Bari King advanced into the bathroom in his boxer shorts. Cool showers of water enlivened his spirits. Stepping out of the bathroom, he confronted Nengi's downcast posture. With her jaw cupped by her right arm, she sat on the bed. He ignored her and began to dress up in casual shorts and vest. He ambulated round the bed, away from Nengi, and stretched out to the bed. The air conditioned surrounding helped to uplift his ease, and the relaxing comforts of the bed provided a sound platform for him to dream away. His thoughts wandered back to his last moments in his jungle encampment. He felt a void within himself which could not be filled by whatever comforts his new abode would offer. He questioned himself and wondered if he missed the freedom of the jungle. Feelings of nostalgia swept across his entire being, and he closed his eyes.

"The food is here," revealed Nengi in a subdued tone, without altering her posture.

"I'm not hungry anymore; I just want to sleep," replied Bari King in a tame voice, with eyes still shut.

"But you said you were hungry not long ago," uttered Nengi, rising up abruptly from the bed, with a face slightly flushed with anger.

He remained almost motionless on the bed and did not vent further words.

She gazed at him with a mixture of sadness and anger. She turned away and began to walk out of the room with enervated motions. As the door closed after her, Bari King opened his eyes and began to gaze at the whiteness of the ceiling. Unfulfilled feelings rumbled inside him, and he closed his eyes once more.

After some minutes, she reentered their bedroom and beheld Bari King's sleeping posture. She made an exit again and decided to go downstairs and watch some television. The images on the television screen failed to capture her attention. Many words, yearning to be embodied into physicality, bounced around in her mind. She shifted around on her chair and resented her unease.

As two hours elapsed, she rose up impatiently from her chair and began to ascend the stair case. The background sound of the television filtered into her ears and still failed to distract her. Entering their bedroom, she cast her gaze on Bari King, who was sitting on the bed. The faraway expression in his eyes did not respond to Nengi's presence.

"Bari is this how we are going to celebrate our reunion, after all these months of separation," expressed Nengi in a controlled voice.

"You are the one setting the tone for everything that is happening," replied Bari King calmly.

"Bari, how do you mean?" queried Nengi in a pained cadence.

"Search within yourself," stated Bari King.

"There is nothing to see," asserted Nengi firmly.

"Then leave me alone, if there's nothing to see," he pronounced.

"Bari, quit talking like that, I'm still your woman," declared Nengi.

"If you are still my woman, then act like one," voiced Bari King. He stirred on the bed and gazed into Nengi's eyes. She searched his countenance but was unable to decipher the expression in his eyes.

Unsympathetic to the overwhelming sad look in her eyes, Bari King turned away and stretched out on the bed.

With a drooping countenance, Nengi veered away and began to walk out of the bedroom. Aware of her sadness that sapped her energy away, she exacted herself on the staircase.

Ignoring the images and sounds of the television set, she collapsed on a sofa in the living room. Doubts stealthily crept into her mind and tormented her with several images. In a bid to distract her mind, she rose up from the sofa and ambled towards the kitchen. She opened the refrigerator and retrieved a bottle of cold water. As she drained the glass, she hoped for the coolness of the water to soothe her innards. Dropping the empty glass, she caught sight of two food flasks, still resting on a marble top. She shrugged her shoulders, and still underscored the infallibility of her actions in her mind. She walked back to the living room and sat down on the sofa. She focused on the television screen and hoped that it would steer her attention away from her oppressive feelings.

Sound of activity in the kitchen filtered into her ears and distracted her from the television. Rising up with a curious expression, she promenaded towards the kitchen.

"Bari, why are you eating biscuits?" queried Nengi calmly.

"For now, I'm not interested in any mass produced food," replied Bari King firmly, closing the door of the refrigerator and facing her.

"Is it not better than the biscuits?" continued Nengi with a note of concern.

"I'm not keen on it," maintained Bari King, as he retrieved a biscuit from a packet in his right hand and popped it into his mouth.

Short of words, she stood by the doorway and glared angrily

at her boyfriend. Without betraying any emotion, he engaged her eyes. Sighing out aloud, she turned and stormed out of the kitchen.

Reclining on the sofa, she fueled the anger within her with her thoughts. The sound of Bari King's motions in the kitchen tended to infuriate her more, and she tuned-up the volume of the television set in a bid to drown out the sound.

Nengi woke up with a start on the sofa and sat up. She glanced at the wall clock and realized that she had been sleeping for a couple of hours. Having reached out for the remote control, she switched off the television set. With languorous motions, she ascended the staircase and entered the bedroom. She gazed at Bari King's sleeping outline for some fleeting moments and then proceeded to the other end of the bed. As she stretched out on the bed, the quietness of the night compounded her loneliness.

To greet the morning, Nengi flaunted the bright colours of her hopes. She glanced to her left and discovered that Bari King was still sleeping. To alight from the bed and go downstairs became her next focus. She entered the kitchen and began to boil some water with the electric kettle.

Having set the table for breakfast, she stepped backwards and appraised its contents with a satisfied grin. Sitting down on a dining chair, she began to thumb through some fashion magazines.

"You brought out just bread for me; you couldn't even fry some eggs to accompany it," voiced Bari King, staring at the contents of the table with a displeased expression.

"Why are you so unappreciating?" remarked Nengi, drawing her attention away from the glossy magazine and glowering at Bari King.

"I want to feel at home; I want some home cooking around me," declared Bari King firmly.

"If you want some home cooking, go and hire a cook," retorted Nengi angrily.

"Hire a cook?" he blurted with an unpleasant frown.

"Yes, hire a cook," maintained Nengi.

"Where are all these defiance coming from?" he queried with a puzzled expression.

"Things are going downhill anyway; you moved to this insignificant house and disposed of most of your vehicles, without bothering about my feelings," stated Nengi.

"Things have definitely changed; and you better adapt to the new situation," he affirmed.

"Adapt to what? This unremarkable house and the new season of lack!" exclaimed Nengi distastefully, rising up from the dining chair and storming away.

The features of Bari King's face assumed a ruminating pose as he gazed into space, away from Nengi's direction.

Glare of the afternoon penetrated into the living room. Bari King reclined on the sofa and indulged in a mid-afternoon reverie.

"Bari, I'm tired of my vehicle, can I have a new one," voiced Nengi in a warmhearted tone, distracting him from his preoccupation and sitting down beside him.

"What is wrong with your vehicle? It is barely one year old," he replied in an unaffected tone, facing ahead.

"Well, I'm just tired of it; reveling in the scent of a new car won't be a bad idea," She continued with a coquettish smile.

"You have to make do with your vehicle; I'm not buying a new one," blurted Bari King firmly.

"Bari, you have never answered me with this kind of vehemence before," she replied, posturing her face sadly.

With a blank expression, he glanced at her for a fleeting second and turned away.

Rising up from the sofa and taking a few steps, she stopped in her tracks and turned towards him.

"Bari, can we at least take a break and go out," said Nengi in an entreating tone.

"Take a break? I just got here," answered Bari King with a baffled expression.

"Can we just go out and eat," she expressed.

"Right now, home is where I want to be," affirmed Bari King emphatically.

"All we do is just fight," stated Nengi, shaking her head despondently.

"And who's to be blamed?" asked Bari King, turning towards her with an accusing look.

"Bari, I don't mind taking all the blame, but please let's make some compromise," entreated Nengi.

"Well, I don't know where you're headed to, but I want to make one thing clear- making a habit of eating outside will never appeal to me," professed Bari King.

"What is wrong in hiring a cook?" she expressed, raising her eyebrows to further underscore her position.

"A cook? Just for two of us!" he ejaculated, slightly raising his voice.

"What is wrong with that?" she defended.

"You must be kidding me," he averred with a grin that mirrored his feelings.

"Bari, I want to look my best for you always; cooking will disfigure my manicured nails; I'm certain that we can afford a cook," she canvassed.

"I won't buy into that," he reechoed.

Turning away from him, she hugged a dejected expression as

she walked towards the staircase. Forespent, she scaled the staircase and entered their bedroom. To placate the sour feelings that plagued her bosom, she stretched out on the bed and gazed at the whiteness of the ceiling.

Evening's light subdued the atmosphere, as Bari King opened the door of their bedroom.

"I'm not feeling well, "stated Nengi in a strained voice, as she stirred tiredly on the bed and turned towards his direction.

He paused in his tracks and turned towards her with a concerned expression.

"What's the problem?" he asked in a mellow voice, drawing closer to her

"I'm feeling very weak," she complained in a drained tone.

"Should we go to the Hospital?' he volunteered sitting down on the bed.

"No! My ailment is emotional in nature; I'll be okay when I feel better," she revealed.

Short of words, he cupped his jaw for some fleeting seconds and rose up from the bed. Unable to temper her weary feelings, she focused at his departing out line.

Emanations from Nengi's gloomy countenance threatened the cheerful light of the morning.

"Bari, I'm leaving," stated Nengi in a gloomy tone as she stood before him.

He dropped the newspaper in his hands on the dining table and critically scrutinized her face.

"I won't stand in your way, if that's your choice," replied Bari King with a vacant expression.

"Is that all you have to say?" voiced Nengi, contorting her face with displeasure.

"I don't know what you expect me say," he replied shrugging

169

his shoulders and directing a questioning glance at her.

"You are really showing that you don't care about me," she accused

"Do you want me to start shedding tears because you're leaving?" avouched Bari King, turning away from her and gazing into space.

"So you're not going to miss me at all?" she expressed, parting her eyelids forcefully.

"Your going is entirely your decision," voiced Bari King.

"How can it be? You have been intentionally making things difficult for me; well, congrats! You have succeeded; I cannot cope with the austerity measures you're implementing around you," she remarked, nodding her head suspiciously.

Her chest heaved up and down as she glowered at him. She channeled the full vent of her anger into her scorching gaze. Coming from the direction of the main entrance gate, sound of blaring horns of a vehicle distracted her. Turning towards entrance door, she walked towards it and opened it.

"Let the vehicle in," shouted Nengi, as she strained towards the security man.

She acknowledged the finger prints left on the atmosphere of the compound by the sound of the maneuvering vehicle, as she reentered the living room. Her malicious gaze failed to crack Bari King's calm repose.

Picking up her two suitcases, she began to wheel them towards the door. The image she projected still failed to weigh down Bari King's countenance. Quelling the suspicious glint in his eyes, he appraised the dark and well-conditioned Mercedes Benz SUV and shrugged his shoulders indifferently. As Nengi boarded the vehicle, his countenance still betrayed nothing. Reclining on the sofa, he acknowledged that he was truly starting afresh.

Images of Kasi steadily drifted into his mind. He closed his eyes and memories of their remarkable Island abode filled his mind. He pictured her vividly and lingered on her calm and kindly countenance. Enlivening feelings swept through him as he imagined her by his side. He ardently yearned for her true devotion and love.

He stood up and glanced about himself. Shrugging his shoulders in resignation, he acknowledged the stilled atmosphere.

The evening's bestowals were mounting before him.

He strolled about his compound and glanced at his watch.

"Jumbo, where are you?" he spoke through his phone.

"I'm not far from your gate," replied Jumbo.

Few minutes after his call, the sound of a vehicle horn blared outside his gate. He glimpsed a dark Toyota sedan, as it made its entrance into his compound. Under his scrutiny, Jumbo and another comrade emerged from the car.

"So! How has it been?" voiced Bari King, shaking Jumbo's hand warmly.

Good! Boss," he replied with a smile.

"Well! We have to go," he stated, after shaking the other man's hand warmly.

They advanced towards the car and boarded it. They were relaxed in each other's company, as they sped along the road. They reached Wimpey Junction and maneuvered into Iwofe road. Gazing out of the window, Bari King observed the evening traffic, which was beginning to build on the adjacent lane. He gazed with consternation at a group of army and police officers, who were clambering down from their Toyota pickup truck. Appraising them critically, he concluded that they were not bothered by the fact that they were moving against the normal run of traffic. He resented them for harassing lawful motorists and rudely herding them to the roadside. He was not far off from the commotion, and he sat up on his chair and peered closely at the marauding convoy. He shook his head disdainfully, when he realized that they were only escorting some European expatriate workers. His anger escalated when he sighted a female motorist, as she lost control of her vehicle and drove into a nearby gutter, due to the hostile action of the officers.

"Don't leave the road and don't listen to them," directed Bari King firmly, lowering the side glass and gazing at the officers, who were crowding around the vehicle in front of their own car. The driver of the vehicle failed to muster enough courage, and with uncomplimentary motions of their hands, the security officers waved the motorist to the roadside.

"What are you still waiting for?" barked the lead policeman, as he advanced menacingly towards the driver's side of Bari King's vehicle.

11

Ill intentions brazenly flashed in the eyes of the aggressive policeman, as he focused on the driver of Bari King's vehicle. The leather whips welded by the security officers cast an ominous light upon them.

As few seconds separated the policeman from Bari King's vehicle, Bari King suddenly burst out of the vehicle with eyes mantled by a defiant expression.

"What do you want?" queried Bari King, as he boldly confronted the policeman.

"Are you so mad that you don't care about your wellbeing," blurted the policeman angrily, as he made to strike Bari King with his leather whip but was restrained with firm nudges from a fellow officer.

"You are the one that is mad; you must be crazy to be driving against the normal run of traffic," replied Bari King, standing his ground.

As the policeman turned towards his colleague with a questioning look in his eyes, his comrade whispered into his ears.

"Do you think I care who you are?" stated the policeman as he glared at Bari King with a boorish expression.

"That whip you're welding; who is it meant for? The civilians you swore to protect? You're quite unfit to be in that police uniform because you don't know what police work is all about; you're recklessly endangering the people you're supposed to protect because you are escorting Italian expatriate workers. Ask those Italians if they can act this lawlessly in their own country. Time of reckoning is coming very soon for your type, Nigeria is gradually changing," voiced Bari King with a dauntless stance.

"The amnesty program will not protect you for very long; you'll see," threatened the police man, as he was being cajoled away by his colleagues.

A triumphant smile played on the features of Bari King's face, as he gazed at the retreating officers. Smiles of admiration mantled the faces of onlookers, who gathered around the scene.

"You did well sir; standing up to them the way you did; it was quite inspiring," voiced a young man, walking up to him and applauding with the expression in his eyes too.

He nodded his head in acknowledgement and returned his attention to the convoy, as it maneuvered and aligned itself properly on the road.

Guardians of the night remained faithful to it. Lying wide awake on his bed, Bari King missed the night sound of the forest.

Gust of very cold air suddenly swept the room and made him to sit up with a

start. Glancing at the air conditioning unit and discovering that it was still

turned off, he engaged a puzzled expression. Fierce barking sound of a dog

suddenly pierced the atmosphere and he hurriedly alighted from the bed.

Confusion steadily crept into his mind as he descended the staircase, on his way

to the living room, where the sound appeared to be coming from. He furrowed his

forehead as he mentally acknowledged his non-ownership of

any dog. Midway on

the staircase, he was suddenly and forcefully pushed by some unseen hands, and

he fell headlong. He managed to break his fall without any serious injury. As he

sat at the foot of the staircase, his chest heaved forcefully up and down. His

fingers trembling with fear, he glanced about the living room with dull motions.

Eerie quietude enveloped him, and he sought to steady his nerves. The dining

area electricity bulb, flashing on and off, as if someone was toying with its

switch, attracted his attention.

"Who's there?" he managed to blurt out, as he rose up from the floor and focused towards the dining area. His chest pounded away furiously as he tiptoed towards the dining area. Glancing at the concerned switch, he failed to behold any person and was truly disturbed by the phenomenon. The bulb continued to flash on and off. Summoning some courage, he pulled out a dining chair and climbed on top of it. As he reached out for the errant bulb, a blast of cold air set upon his face and heralded a very violent assault by an unseen entity. As he crumpled to the floor, he wondered about the motive behind the violent shoving he received. His striving to rise up from the floor did not yield any fruit. He fell back to the floor. As he began to examine a bruised ankle, a cacophonous and mocking laugher rang out about him. With desperate motions, he scrambled onto his feet and limped away. He ascended the staircase as fast as he could and was still aware of the eerie circumstance created by the flashing light bulb.

The comfortable ambience of his bedroom failed to soothe him and confusion reigned supreme in his mind. His motions were frantic as he glanced about the room. Focusing on the bed, he was convinced that no comfort would materialize from it, so he veered away from it. He hurried into the toilet; and still, his confusion would not let up.

Ambulating back to his bedroom, he welcomed the soundless atmosphere that strove to convince him that normalcy had returned. Cautiously, he walked to the bed and sat down. He cupped his jaw and goaded his thoughts to unravel the oppressive events that assailed him a short while ago. Suspiciously appraising the room, he gently reposed himself on the bed. He glanced at the bedside clock and discovered that it was some minutes after two am. He shook his head woefully, as he acknowledged the unfavorable hour. He toyed with the idea of abandoning his home but later decided against it. Sleepiness set upon him and toyed with his resolve to stay awake. His self-preservation instinct energized him and he fought off sleep. As he finally succumbed to the alluring charms of sleep, his face twitched nervously. His tensed outline adorned his bed.

Barely an hour after he slept off, rough and unseen hands rudely shook him up. He sat up on the bed and his confounded eyes darted about the room apprehensively. He strongly suspected that an attack from the unseen oppressive entity was imminent but was at loss as to where to take cover. His wristwatch suddenly lifted upwards, without any physical aid, from its position on the bedside cabinet. Suspended in midair by some unseen force, it began to gyrate around him, in a macabre dance. He paid scant attention to the whirling wrist watch, and he dared not to breathe deeply, for fear of attracting further onslaughts. Suddenly, the wrist watch landed forcefully on the floor and shattered into pieces. As the last piece of the wrist watch came to rest on the floor, a guttural laughter rang out in the bedroom. Bari King was transfixed on the bed, without any form of mental poise. His fearful state restrained him from blinking his eyes. An overpowering foul odor suddenly seized the atmosphere of his bedroom. Cupping his nose and mouth with the palm of his right hand, he ran into the toilet. Darting his head sideways, he dabbed at his clammy forehead with the back of his palm. Confused and fearful, he stood in the middle of the toilet. Without warning, savage barking sound of an unseen dog invaded the airwaves. Straining his neck, he failed to catch the glimpse of any dog. As the vicious barking increased in intensity and aligned towards his direction, he trembled uncontrollably and began to step backwards. As his back hit the wall, the unfriendly barking sound suddenly ceased, and a guttural laughter rang out in its place. With his back against the wall, his legs turned wobbly, and he caved in. Lying helplessly on the floor, he perceived the rumbling sound of his stomach and felt like relieving his bowels. He restrained himself for fear of provoking more infernal attacks from the unseen entity.

Bari King's apprehensive thoughts were not soothed by the dubious calm that settled over the atmosphere. Without any physical interference and of its own accord, the knob of the cold water, anchored over the bath-tub, began to swirl around. As he viewed the running water, he felt the stinging sensation of tepid perspiration. Under the influence of a similar unseen force, the knob of the wash basin tap began to mirror the motion of that of the bath-tub. The combined sound of running water assaulted his sense of ease and heightened his confusion. Staring ahead, away from the running water, he sought to drown out its sound inside his mind. Counseled wisely by his self-preservation instinct, he decided to leave the running waters alone.

An uneasy calm, ranked very high by Bari King on the infernal scale, suddenly descended upon the ambience of the toilet once more. Without any hint of elation, he noticed that the running waters had become extinct.

Under the burden of heavy silence, he witnessed several minutes. Finally rising weakly to his feet, he ambled out of the toilet, with an air of resignation. Turning towards the bedside clock, he discovered that it was some minutes after four am. Pulling the clammy white t-shirt off his back, he reached towards the wardrobe. Turning his back against the larger expanse of the bedroom nurtured a sense of vulnerability within him. He hastily retrieved a fresh white t-shirt. As he made to wear his t-shirt, some unseen force impeded his effort, and a tug of war ensued between himself and the unseen entity.

"Why don't you show yourself?" voiced Bari King defiantly, still holding onto his t-shirt.

Panting heavily, he finally relinquished his hold on the t-shirt. As the t-shirt hovered in mid-air, a rasping laughter rang out in the bedroom. The white t-shirt floated in midair, and the knob of the toilet door opened of its own accord and permitted the t-shirt to disappear through the door. Watching the toilet door as it returned to its former position, he felt anger welling up within him. Running his hand against his hairy chest, he longed to expel every hint of fear within him.

Mindful of the calmness in the bedroom, he nurtured his defiant disposition. To relieve his bladder, he ambled towards the toilet. Having drawn closer to the water closet, he beheld his white t-shirt, stuffed inside the bowels of the water closet. His face flushed with anger as he defined it in detail. A cacophonous laughter suddenly rang out and startled him away from the soaked white t-shirt. His chest heaving vigorously up and down, he stilled his motion and waited.

After removing the sodden t-shirt from the depths of the water closet, he dumped it inside the bath-tub and relieved his bladder.

Cautious with good reasons, he sauntered into his bedroom. Drained by his experiences, he glanced at the bedside clock and discovered that it was fifteen minutes to five in the morning. Sitting down on the bed, he yawned tiredly. Fatigue and perplexity stole over every other emotion.

Confusion still reigned inside his mind, and he was at loss as to his next line of action. Eventually seduced by sleep, he began to nod his head in surrender. Cautiously, he lifted his legs from the floor and stretched out his frame on the bed. He slept fitfully and kept waking up intermittently.

Clear light of morning finally graced the confines of his bedroom and comforted him, as propped himself against two pillows, on his bed. As he gazed into space, the disconcerting event of the previous night occupied his mind. His thoughts still failed to unravel the mystery behind the strange occurrences. Drained in every fiber of his being, he staggered to his feet and sauntered towards the staircase. He gripped the handrail firmly and descended the staircase with inelegant footsteps. To retrieve a bottle of cold water, he opened the refrigerator in the kitchen. Gulping down a glass of cold water imbued him with some measure of vitality. Promenading back to the staircase, he turned his thoughts towards Jumbo. To call him with his mobile phone became an urgent preoccupation for him. Feeling a noticeable surge of energy within him, he ascended the staircase. He reached out for his mobile handset a soon as he entered his bedroom.

"Jumbo, where are you? I need to talk to you urgently," began Bari King, as he held the mobile phone to his ears.

"Boss, I'm already on my way to your house; I'm not far off; I'll soon be there," replied Jumbo.

"You're on your way to my house?" voiced Bari King in a ruminative tone.

"Sure Boss; I'll soon be there," reiterated Jumbo.

Holding the phone against his cheeks, he permitted a pensive expression to adorn the features of his face. Sitting down on the bed, he gaped into space.

The horn of a car sounded within the vicinity of his main entrance gate, and he suspected that Jumbo was around. Alighting from the bed, he felt some sense of reassurance inspired by his coming. With renewed vigour, he moved down the staircase.

"Jumbo, how has it been?" expressed Bari King shaking him vigorously.

"Boss! It's sure good to see you again," responded Jumbo with a whole hearted smile.

"What of our guys? I hope they are adjusting well," voiced Bari King, with a note of care, as he relaxed his grip.

"They are doing okay," replied Jumbo.

"So why are you up this early?" queried Bari King with keen attention, "please sit down," he added, occupying a sofa.

"Akoju called me on phone early this morning; he stated that they are the ones tormenting you with various ills," revealed Jumbo solemnly.

"I see!" stated Bari King, nodding his head thoughtfully.

"Boss, have you been plagued by any strange phenomenon of late?" queried Jumbo apprehensively.

"Sure! Last night was really hellish," expressed Bari King, mentally striving hard to suppress his rising anxiety.

"Boss, what should we do? He is still threatening that more vicissitudes will follow, if you fail to honor the covenant you made with them," revealed Jumbo, in a concerned tone.

"We need to go and seek out Agila, the famed medicine man," ejaculated Bari King.

"Do you think he can help us?" asked Jumbo.

"It's worth a try," stated Bari King, hopefully.

"Boss, I want you to know that I'm solidly behind you," averred Jumbo, standing up to emphasize his stand.

"Thank you; I know I can always count on you; we will leave immediately; go and pack a light suitcase and come back soonest," articulated Bari King, rising to his feet.

"Sure Boss, I won't take long at all," declared Jumbo as he hurried away from him.

After dishing out instruction to his domestic-worker, he moved up the staircase. He packed a few clothes in a handy travelling bag and ambled into the bathroom. The cold water, trickling down his frame, imbued him with some freshness.

Sitting behind his dining table, he viewed the jollof rice and fried plantain delivered by his domestic help. With his mind focused on his impending journey, he failed to relish the delicious taste of the food.

Blaring horns of a vehicle, seeking entrance into his premises, roused him to full consciousness. He gulped down a glass of water and stood up.

"Jumbo, you're back," he expressed with a genial smile, as Jumbo walked towards him.

"Boss, I'm ready," declared Jumbo with an unwavering tone.

Nodding his head appreciatively, Bari King still nurtured a ruminative expression. Picking up his bag, he headed towards the door, with Jumbo in tow. He entered the front passenger seat and Jumbo sped off. Images of the familiar river and water floated into his mind and drenched him with a keen sense of elation. As the cityscape disappeared behind them, Bari King reclined against the seat of the Toyota Corolla sedan and closed his eyes. He dozed all the way to his country home. The familiar grounds of his premises inspired poignant memories within him. He yawned languorously and stretched his arms. Distracted by the greeting of another comrade, he turned towards him and reciprocated with appreciative nods of his head. Jumbo moved from the driver's seat to the rear seat and their comrade occupied his former position. They hastened away from the compound and oriented themselves towards the jetty. The towering trees on neighboring parcels of land reminded him of his former camp in the forest, and he shook his head wistfully.

With the jetty in close proximity, Bari King and Jumbo alighted from the vehicle and advanced towards it. His simple jean trousers, plain yellow t-shirt, and matching facing cap helped him to conceal his identity. They boarded a waiting white executive launch, and the driver zoomed off. The receding waters and memorable sights brought some measures of poignancy to his emotions. Dark log boats of local fishermen stood out on the waters; deep hopes radiated from their eyes, as they sprayed their nets over the waters.

After about fifty minutes, they sighted he shores of the river. Bari King's heartbeat raced mildly, as he acknowledged Kasi's sharp image, nestling within the confines of his mind. He thought about Agila; and ardently yearned for his co-operation and help. They disembarked from the boat and stepped onto the sandy shores. Clutching their hand bags, they made their way into the untarred road that led into the town. Bari King glanced backwards and beheld the villagers loitering around their fancy white launch, with looks of admiration in their eyes. The shoreline was littered with dark log boats; and some of them were laden with fishes that inoculated the atmosphere with their scent.

With renewed sense of reassurance, Bari King trekked along the dirt road, in Jumbo's company. Villagers, carrying buckets and pans, filled with fishes, periwinkles, crayfish and crabs, shared the road with them. Bari King glanced at them, from time to time, and envied the contented expression on some of their faces. Kasi's image loomed large in his mind, once more, and he invested a part of his consciousness in thoughts of her.

Standing before the familiar steel pedestrian gate of Agila's compound, he felt his heartbeat, as it gathered more speed. Comforted by Jumbo's loyalty, he glanced at him appreciatively. Sandy beaches, dotted with swaying coconut trees, loomed ahead of him and inspired more ease in his feelings. Mild pressure exerted by his fingers pried the gate open. The sight of Agila, sitting on an easy wooden chair and arranging some herbs and roots, greeted him. The unexcited genial expression on his face heartened Bari King as they ambled towards him.

"We greet you sir," began Bari King courteously, as they stood before him.

"I welcome you and your friend," responded Agila in a friendly tone, withdrawing his hands from the bunch of herbs, "Kasi, bring two chairs for our visitors," he voiced, turning towards the entrance door of his living room. Sound occasioned by the interaction of household items filtered into their ears.

An air of supplication dominated his bearing, as Bari King engaged Agila's calm countenance. Kasi emerged from the living room, clutching two white plastic chairs. At the sight of her, Bari King dropped his bag and hurried towards her.

"'Let me take the chairs," volunteered Bari King, reaching out for the chairs, without giving her an option.

"Good day," greeted kasi, relinquishing her hold on the chairs.

"Good day to you too," responded Bari King cheerfully, "and thank you for the chairs," he added.

"You're welcome ," voiced Kasi with a polite smile, as she turned away from him.

"Please bring drinks for us," requested Agila, turning towards Kasi.

"Yes, father," responded Kasi.

Boss, let me have the chairs," expressed Jumbo, standing in front of Bari King.

"It's okay; I'll carry them," maintained Bari King, with a cordial smile.

He positioned the chairs in front of Agila and they sat down. Shortly afterwards, Kasi placed a bottle of locally brewed gin, and three tumblers on the empty table before them. Her presence instigated stimulating warmth that enlivened Bari King. Agila poured drinks for all of them and then reclined on his chair. Nursing his glass, Agila gazed thoughtfully at Bari King.

"Things are different now compared to the last time I visited you," verbalized Bari King meekly.

"Yes, I gathered that," replied Agila, underscoring his words with gentle nods of his head.

"Frankly, I'm in trouble right now," blurted Bari King, gazing pensively at his glass.

"I can see that; there's a trail of darkness terminating around you," stated Agila calmly.

"How do you mean?" queried Bari King, widening his eyes with alarm and setting down his glass.

"Never mind!" uttered Agila.

"What do you see that I can't see?" continued Bari King with rising apprehension.

Agila sipped his drink and reclined on his chair. His expression was serious, yet gentle, as he regarded Bari King.

"You allowed your drive for power to override all your internal alarm systems; you chose a path that shrouded you in a web of darkness," voiced Agila calmly.

"Please can you explain further," entreated Bari King, sitting up and setting his glass on the table. His energy dissipating away, he felt his stomach as it knotted up.

"You know exactly what I'm talking about," posited Agila.

Bari King became thoughtful for some seconds and then raised his head.

"Are you referring to the covenant of protection I made?" he asked with trepidation.

"You're right on target," replied Agila with a smile.

"Please help me; I'm renouncing everything; I just want to live a peaceful and unassuming life now," pleaded Bari King, leaning fervently towards him.

"Your current desires are quite noble, but how are you going to resolve your past entanglements," expressed Agila.

"Please help me!" blurted Bari King.

"Can I really be of help to you? Asked Agila rhetorically, looking away from him, "you are the one holding the key to salvaging yourself," he added, gazing at him.

"Please tell me more," affirmed Bari King.

"The sincerity of your resolution is more important than my words," expressed Agila.

"Please tell me what to do,"' averred Bari King as he flashed the eagerness that mantled his eyes.

"Are you certain of that?" stated Agila.

"I won't be here if I didn't trust you," asserted Bari King.

The features of Agila's face attained a ruminative pose, as he focused at Bari King.

"This journey is for you alone; you need to let go of your companion," directed Agila.

Motioning at Jumbo with his head, Bari King rose up from his chair. After conferring privately with Jumbo, he walked back to his chair. Jumbo picked up his own bag and ambled towards the gate.

"Hand over your bag to your friend as well," advised Agila.

"Jumbo, please take my bag," requested Bari King, gazing towards Jumbo's direction.

Turning towards him, Jumbo nodded his head in accent and took custody of his bag.

A mellow light prevailed on the atmosphere, as Agila rose upwards. He glanced skywards and nodded his head with satisfaction.

"Kasi," he called.

"Yes father," she answered, emerging from the living room.

"We are going into the forest," stated Agila.

"Father, go well and return in peace," voiced Kasi.

He nodded his head appreciatively and turned towards an outbuilding within the same premises.

Kasi's fleeting thoughtful glance graced Bari King's direction, before she turned towards the entrance door of their living room.

He earnestly hoped that she caught a glimpse of the radiant light painted on the canvass provided by his eyes. Gazing at her departing outline, he imagined how wonderful it would be to have her in his living space.

"It's time for us to go," interjected Agila, interrupting his inner reverie, "leave that small bag behind, Kasi will take care of it," he continued.

He stood up and appraised Agila. His simple wrapper, white t-shirt, and goatskin bag hung about his shoulders failed to mirror the future.

Agila ambled towards the entrance gate, with Bari King very close on his heels. They took a footpath and walked for about six minutes, before they reached the edge of the forest. The towering Iroko trees with their massive trunks made pronounced impressions on Bari King. Crunching sound emitted as their legs impacted on the dry and desiccated leaves on the forest floor formed an accompanying symphony. Brightly colored parrots chirped away and cheered agile monkeys and they darted from one tree to the other. They trekked for about thirty-five minutes inside the forest and stopped in front of a hut constructed with bamboo stems and thatched roof. Agila opened the door and led the way. With a trustful air, he followed him into the hut. Agila opened two windows and allowed light to penetrate inside the hut. Standing on fresh banana leaves, he observed the neat and uncluttered space.

"Sit down and wait for me; I'll be back in a few minutes," voiced Agila, retiring his goatskin bag at a corner of the hut and walking towards the door.

As the door closed behind Agila's back, Bari King glanced about him and felt quite reassured in Agila's care. He sat down opposite the goatskin bag and wondered about its contents.

Clutching some fresh leaves and newly harvested bulbs, with remnants of earth still clinging on them, Agila appeared after some few minutes. Without uttering any word to Bari King, he calmly advanced towards his goatskin bag and retrieved a bamboo receptacle. With curious eyes, he observed Agila as he walked out of the hut again. Outside the hut, Agila washed the leaves and bulbs that appeared strange to Bari King.

Under the serene ambience of the hut, Agila brought out a

portable bamboo mortar and wooden pestle from his goatskin bag. After stuffing the leaves and bulbs inside the mortar and introducing a little water, he began to mash them with the pestle. With increasing inquisitiveness, Bari King peered at him and wondered about the next step that would follow.

After some minutes, Agila examined and weighed the contents of the bamboo mortar and adjudged them okay.

"I believe you accompanied me to this place because of your unwavering trust in me; allow your inner state to continue to nurture that trust; it would help you in this journey you are about to embark with me," voiced Agila. as he turned towards Bari King.

"I will faithfully follow all your instructions," reassured Bari King firmly. The banana leaves crackled as he shifted his weight on them and nodded emphatically.

"It's now time," stated Agila calmly, approaching Bari King with the mixed paste in his care, "spirits of heaven and earth, we stand here with a genuine desire to know ourselves; please protect and guide us with your luminous light," continued Agila as he looked past Bari King.

Silently, Agila offered the mixed paste, contained in the bamboo mortar, to the four directions. Motioning for Bari King to open his hand, he delivered the greenish paste onto the palm of his right hand. With a calm disposition, Bari King gazed at the cool paste on his palm and then turned towards Agila.

"Go ahead and chew on it; extract the moisture and spit out the rest; chew it for about ten minutes," counseled Agila calmly.

He nodded in the affirmative and delivered the paste into his mouth.

"Stretch out on the floor; relax yourself, and place your arms against your sides," continued Agila, gazing at Bari King and depositing some of the paste into his own mouth.

He positioned himself on the floor beside Bari King and closed his eyes.

"Do not be afraid of the sensations you'll experience; try to relax and let go of yourself," reassured Agila as he patted him on his legs.

Gazing at Agila's calm outline, he focused briefly at his closed eyes and then veered away from him. He closed his eyes and wondered about the next step. Suddenly, Bari King opened his eyes and leaned upwards with hands anchored firmly on the ground.

"Please relax yourself and surrender to the sensations; observe your fear and accept it; know that your greater self is greater than this fear," soothed Agila, who was roused by the vibrant cracking of the banana leaves under Bari King.

Gently, Bari King rested his frame back on the banana leaves. Feelings of weightlessness, and a sinking sensation still possessed him. His unfamiliar sensations were gradually drawing his consciousness away from the symphonic chirping of birds outside their enclosure.

Still stretched out on the floor, he became aware of Agila's motions. Agila advanced towards his goatskin bag and retrieved a portable drum and stick. He walked back to his position and sat down. Striking the drum in a rhythmic sequence, he closed his eyes. The rhythmic drum beats heightened the sinking sensations and feelings of weightlessness within Bari King. He earnestly aligned himself to Agila's counsel.

The rhythmic drum beats suddenly faded away and Bari King suddenly found himself in an upright position inside the bamboo hut. He felt strangely unfamiliar. His lightness of being amazed him. He shuddered with alarm as he gazed at himself. He noticed that he still had a human form but the colour of his body was grayish. Glancing about himself, he flinched with increased alarm as he beheld his physical body still stretched out on the floor. He lowered his frame and attempted to touch it but is hands went through his physical body without creating any sensation of touch. He straightened his frame and observed himself once more. He touched himself and felt solidity. He peered at himself with closer attention and discovered that there were points of light, glowing at different levels of intensity scattered about his frame. The light somewhat clarified his grayish complexion. He wondered why the light below his navel was dimmer than he ones at the upper part of his new body. Thoughts of Agila suddenly animated the landscape of his mind. Glancing about himself, he beheld Agila by his side.

"Have you been standing here all along?" queried Bari King curiously.

"Yes," answered Agila, without parting his mouth.

"How come I'm hearing you when you are not opening your mouth?" he continued.

"You are no longer in your physical body, and when that happens, thoughts become everything; in other words, thoughts become deed," replied Agila calmly.

"Can I do that too?"asked Bari King curiously.

"Yes of course, it does not require any special talent; it is spiritual law," declared Agila.

"Why are you radiating more light than myself?" inquired Bari King.

"You will find out by yourself," projected Agila.

"Are you telling me everything? You suddenly appeared at my side," intuited Bari King inside his mind, as he experimented with the new concept.

"I was by your side all the while, but you did not perceive me because you focused all your attention and thoughts on yourself," projected Agila.

"We are not dead I hope?"queried Bari King, reassured by Agila's presence.

"No we are not," intuited Agila.

"So what happens to our physical bodies?" projected Bari King, glancing at their motionless bodies, stretched out on the banana leaves.

"Don't worry about them; they are safe," reassured Agila.

"Your white tunic, where did you get it," queried Bari King, appraising his own Jeans and t-shirt.

"I created it with my thoughts," communicated Agila.

"That's interesting," declared Bari King, with an excited countenance.

"You are still in your jeans and t-shirt because of your expectations; you can create another attire for yourself if you wish," transmitted Agila.

"How can I do that?" queried Bari King, with a curious glint about his eyes.

"Just picture yourself in any attire of your liking and it would become deed immediately," volunteered Agila with a kind smile.

"Okay! I will give it a try," enthused Bari King, closing his eyes. After some intervening moments, he opened his eyes and appraised himself. As a matter of fact, he withdrew his eyes with clear disappointment written all over his face and turned towards Agila.

"It's not working out for me," he ejaculated.

"Your doubts got in the way, by observing the feelings connected to your doubts, you free yourself from obsessing about them and actually allow them to proceed on their natural course.

Afterwards, repeat this statement three times: Iam one with the universe, and Iam the power of the universe. Then, relax and picture what you desire, counseled Agila."

"Uumm! Okay," projected Bari King, closing his eyes. After some moments, he opened his eyes and surveyed himself; a big smile broke across his face, as he acknowledged his grey tunic,

"So where did the jeans and t-shirt disappear to?" he asked.

"In this reality; everything is energy, and you use your attention and desire to coalesce it together; your jeans and t-shirt disappeared because you no longer expected them to be in your reality," conveyed Agila.

"It is getting quite interesting, though I'm not yet as bright as you." beamed Bari King.

"It's time for us to move on," posited Agila calmly; "just focus your attention on me, with the intention of accompanying me," he continued.

"How did this happen?" queried Bari King with animated eyes as he glanced at the towering trees, "how did we suddenly appear outside the hut; I didn't feel any travelling sensation," he continued.

A powerful and unfamiliar presence suddenly instigated jolting sensations within Bari King. Turning to his right, he beheld a figure that challenged his imagination. Awestricken, he stepped backwards and narrowed the space between himself and Agila. With a tame expression, he directed a questioning look at Agila. However, the relaxed expression on Agila's face allayed all his fears and suspicions.

"He is my spiritual ally," mentally intoned Agila, as he calmly gazed at the being.

Appraising the being, Bari King suspected that his height would be close to seven feet. His spotted skin reminded him of a jaguar. With a good dose of wonder, he noticed that his anatomy mirrored that of a man but his eyes, nose, mouth and whiskers resembled those of a jaguar. The expression on his face, which was neither mirthful nor stern, did not scare him. He found his sturdy physique quite inspiring. The being's penetrating gaze bored right through him and forced him to cringe. In addition, he lowered his head and turned towards Agila.

The jaguar man suddenly disappeared and materialized in front of the hut. He stretched his hand towards the hut, and a roseate gossamer canopy suddenly enveloped the hut. The enchanting colours of the canopy captured Bari Kings attention. A grey masculine being, without hands and legs, suddenly emerged from a nearby Iroko tree and loomed before him.

"Ahhh!" ejaculated Bari King with terror as he dashed towards Agila.

"Every tree in this forest has a spiritual guardian; you just got yourself introduced to the non-physical keeper of the Iroko tree," educated Agila.

Glancing at the Iroko tree and neighboring trees, he was struck by their lively hues.

"Your body and the energies they radiate is the book of your life; only you can save yourself," intoned the jaguar being telepathically; as he focused intently at Bari King,.

Turning towards the other worldly jaguar being, Bari King was enamored by the power that oozed from the being his message. His iridescent spots sparkled and blotted all doubts inside Bari King's mind. With a curious disposition, Bari King veered towards Agila. Agila's calm countenance failed to placate his curiosity; and he made a detour once more. A bewildered expression tugged at the contours of his face, as he realized that the jaguar being had disappeared. Furiously, he glanced about himself and then submitted to the situation.

"Focus your attention on me," advised Agila.

As soon as Bari King complied with his directive, they materialized in another realm. Bari King marveled at the exquisite highway that led into the realm. The highway exuded a beautiful colour that he had never seen on earth. Well proportioned trees and flowers in full bloom lined the highway. The animated flowers seemed to be communicating pleasantly to his mind. He leaned towards an enchanting rose flower. The flower tilted towards him and filled him with warmth.

"The flowers are communicating with me!" exclaimed Bari King, as he turned towards Agila.

"It's time for us to go," interjected Agila patiently.

"Okay," replied Bari King, reluctantly drawing himself away from the captivating flowers.

They materialized inside an open auditorium that was filled with beings that appeared human in appearance. Bari King surveyed the crowd and was impressed by the friendly expressions on their faces. The light about them radiated very inspiring colors. He admired their simple tunic and barefooted mode of being. The gathering was a mixture of different races; he acknowledged Whites, Orientals, and Blacks. The common denominator they shared was the uplifting light that enveloped their entire being. Bari King and Agila stood at the rear and responded to the warm smiles directed at them by incoming patrons. Striding along a passage way, a man approached them. He paused before them and offered a genial smile. He then focused his attention on Agila. From the expressions on their faces, Bari King suspected that they were engaged in a nonverbal communication with some measure of familiarity.

"Please come this way," requested the man telepathically, as he gazed at Bari King.

The man led the way and they followed him. He paused and pointed to two vacant seats at the lowest terrace.

"Were they expecting us?" asked Bari King, as he puckered his face with curiosity and riveted his attention on the center stage.

His intentness still unalloyed, he gazed at several drums, which were of different hues that surrounded a lone man on the stage. He wore a white tunic like most of the people and radiated very inspiring colors, some of which he had never seen before. His calm and peaceful disposition touched a longing deep within him.

"How's he going to play all those drums?" asked Bari King, still fascinated by the spectacle on stage.

"Just watch," replied Agila, also concentrating on the stage.

Bari King's attention strayed to the cheerful sky. Still failing to see the source of its illumination, he welcomed its soothing rays. A most calming and rhythmic sound suddenly caressed his soul and redirected his attention back to the stage. He noticed that all the drums were vibrating at the same time without any physical contact with the performer. He shook his head and marveled at the phenomenon that was unfolding before him.

"How is he managing to do that? To beat all the drums at the same time without having any contact with them?" ruminated Bari King inside his mind.

"He used the power of his thoughts and intention to suspend the drums around himself and animate them simultaneously!" responded Agila.

"Fascinating!" ejaculated Bari King, still immersed in the inner bliss inspired by the rhythm of the drums.

"What is that above the man's head?" he continued, focusing his attention on a bluish form that resembled a flower in luxurious bloom. Its countless tints, which flaunted some strange enchanting colours, enthralled him. Enraptured, he noticed that the beautiful form responded to the crescendo of the drum beat.

"Every musical rhythm creates a subtle form that is invisible to the physical eyes; the more harmonious the music is; the more refined and beautiful its form will be," underscored Agila.

Bari King immersed himself in the harmonious and enchanting rhythm of the drums. The concept of time, as he knew it before, vanished from his mind. The soothing sensation inspired by the melodious drum beats was quite incredible, and they appeared to be penetrating right into his very soul. The performer barely lifted his hand, and just moved his head sideways, in alignment with the positions of the drums. Immersed in the harmonious rhythm, he forgot about the disappointment engendered by his dim emanations.

"We have to go, "intruded Agila.

"This is quite some experience; can we stay for some more?" replied Bari King as he practiced his new found telepathic skills.

"It's time to go," maintained Agila.

"Okay," projected Bari king, reluctantly withdrawing his attention from the spectacle on the stage.

An unfamiliar and hospitable environment suddenly unfolded before Bari King. Glancing about himself, he welcomed Agila's reassuring presence. His eyes lit up, as he focused on giant and exquisite white rose flowers that surrounded them. The grassy plain, on which they stood, offered a velvety cushion to their legs. Brightly coloured birds, the types he had never seen before, fluttered here and there, and danced before them.

"The birds are communicating with me too," blurted Bari King, in amazement, "I feel their warmth and love," he continued.

Gazing upwards at the bright and enchanting Sky, he welcomed its loving rays, working in consonance with their uplifting surroundings.

The beautiful bloom of a rose flower suddenly sparkled, as a delicate and lovely female being emerged from it. The being glided in midair and landed before them. Entranced by the intense loving energy emanating from the being, Bari King focused completely on her. Other beings of like species gathered about her and formed a semicircle. Their forms were entirely luminous. A kaleidoscope of beautiful colours bubbled at the core of their hearts and expanded outwards, heightening the ecstatic impact of their loving goodwill.

"This kind of love! How is it possible?" pondered Bari King inside his mind. The magic of their presence still elicited wonder in his eyes.

"His dark threads are too dense; we cannot anchor on them and transmute them," projected the first being, still flaunting a balanced mixture of gentleness and seriousness.

"She must be talking about me," ruminated Bari King. A wave of disappointment crashed inside his mind and dented his beatific feelings. Looking for solace, he searched through the firm and unwavering eyes of the being. Loss of some imagined goodness plagued him.

The sinking feeling and feeling of weightlessness suddenly returned; and everything around him became fuzzy. Alarmed, he turned towards Agila and discovered that his outline was fading from his view.

"What is happening?" he bemoaned with rising trepidation.

A grey and misty realm sudden enveloped him. Plagued by confusion, he darted his eyes about himself and was greeted by muffled and desolate cries. Scattered about him were grey-complexioned men and women. Stifled points of light clung to their bodies and were noticeable through their tattered clothes.

Steadily, the stifling environment of the bleak and misty realm got to him and he began to gasp for breath. Mindful of his own discomfiture, he discovered that the cries of the other inhabitants of the realm were a mixture of anguish and desperate gasping motions. Doubling up and dropping to his knees with a contorted face, he was startled by a guttural and mocking laughter. Peering through the mist, he encountered a monstrous being that froze his motions. He galvanized all his inner resources to quell the fear that possessed him. The shanty abode of the monstrous being added to the eerie nature of the realm. Bari King steeled himself, as the grotesque being approached him. The being was dark and big. Its worn clothing highlighted its muscular frame. Bloodshot eyes and a cancerous opening in the position of a nose defined the entity. Four other dark beings and a four legged ugly creature trailed behind it. The imperial swagger of the monstrous entity proclaimed him as the lord of the realm.

"Ha! Ha! Ha!" cackled the entity, as it leered towards Bari King, "You think you'll get away from me; welcome home to daddy," it jeered, flashing its eyes ominously at him.

"Ummh! Are you not afraid of me?" queried the monster in an infernal tone, as he stepped backwards to appraise him.

With his head thrust backwards, in a bid to escape from the breath of the monster, Bari King presented a very blank expression on his face.

"You will now bow to me, as the lord of this realm," commanded the entity, with features that were held together with ominous lines.

"I will not do such thing," responded Bari King boldly, tightening his fists to prevent them from trembling.

Baring its needlelike teeth, the four legged ill-looking creature began to snarl viciously at him. It appeared to be privy to the verbal exchange between Bari King and the misshapen entity.

"First, you approached me and entered a covenant with me. Thereafter, you reneged on your obligations; now you are in my domain and you're refusing to acknowledge me. Grrrrr! Do you really know where you are" thundered the entity.

Boldly engaging the animated bloodshot eyes of the entity, Bari King still nurtured a defiant expression.

"There's no escape for you here- only more pain; death can't even rescue you, I'll teach you who's Boss around here, ha! Ha! Ha! Ha!" ejaculated the monster ominously. With evil intentions, his dark companions emitted malevolent grunts, and the four legged creature imbued vigour to its motions, as it antagonized Bari King with his growls.

The air was thick with the fearful and anguished cries of other inhabitants of the grey and misty realm. The monster surveyed the inconsolable humanity of his domain and nodded his head with satisfaction. The lewd smile on its face withered away, as his gaze settled once more on Bari King. Unmitigated anger invigorated its blood-shot eyes, as he glared at him. Turning towards the four-legged creature was an obvious signal, and it immediately pounced on Bari King with lightening speed. Surprised by its swiftness, Bari King reeled under its incredible weight. The smell from its hairy body was nauseating to him. His energy began to dissipate away as it sank its needlelike teeth into his neck. After a desperate struggle, he mustered all his inner resources and threw it off him. Rising up briskly, he rebuffed another attack from the creature. Growling fiendishly, the beast lunged at him again. and he managed to beat off the attack. In obedience to a hand signal from his master, the beast halted in its track and began to snarl viciously at Bari King.

He observed that his determination and intention to fend off the beast drew more vitality to him. His breathing improved tremendously as he paid scant attention to the grey and misty atmosphere.

"This is just a tip of what you'll be enjoying here, urrh! Ha! Ha! Ha! Ha!" derided the monster. Glancing at the frightful gathering of men and women, the horrid being grinned gleefully and turned away with his train.

Some distance separated him from the monster's band, but the infernal snarl of the four legged beast still reverberated in his consciousness, as if it was standing before him. He scanned his body and discovered that there was no visible wound. Bari King lifted his head with relief and turned towards his right. Preoccupied mutterings of his nearest neighbor, made more bizarre by his desperate gasps for breath, failed to hold his attention. The man's tattered mantle forced him into a moment of deep reverie, and he contemplated his fate.

"Why did Agila abandon me?" he ruminated ruefully, "and how can I escape from this terrible place," he continued. He resolved never to succumb to his fears and bow down before the dark monster. He glanced at his grey tunic and was heartened that it did not mirror the tattered spectacle that pervaded the realm.

The grotesque monster paced up and down inside its shanty abode. Its abode had no windows, and the atmosphere was dark with very little visibility. There were no furnishings to impede his ill-humoured footsteps. His men pressed their backs against the wall, away from the space he dominated, as a precautionary measure against his fury. Their eyes shone with their desire to conform to whatever order he issued.

"Grrr! That man is no ordinary visitor; we must break him before he spoils everything," seethed the being.

"Master! We're ready to serve you; just command us," chorused the men, as they knelt down before the entity.

"We must instill fear in him and force him to succumb to it; fear is my ultimate weapon; it is what I will use to blunt his spiritual eyes and bind him eternally to this realm, ha! ha! ha! ha!" vociferated the entity, with enlivened bloodshot eyes, "You men must not disappoint me," it asseverated, enveloping the men with his foul breath.

"We are at your command; we live to please you," affirmed the men.

"Get going now," commanded the entity. The men scrambled to their feet and headed towards an opening that acted as an entrance into the dimly lit shack.

"He inadvertently stumbled on a secret that could bring everything to ruin; use all available means to brutalize and remind him that I'm the only Boss and lord of this realm," it added in a crazed guttural tone.

Appraising his environs and failing to draw out any grain of inspiration from it, Bari King turned away from it and focused his attention on the four dark grey men that approached him. Their hefty build highlighted the malevolent intentions that shone from their eyes. He clenched his fists and readied himself. Palpable tension broadcasted across the length of his entire being. Their villainous smiles only emboldened his resolve to stand his ground and not bow to his fear. With heightened apprehension, he realized that the men had suddenly dematerialized from his view. He braced himself for the inevitable onslaught, he suspected would follow. Four swords and spears suddenly appeared before him. Few meters away from him and of their own accord, they danced in mid air to some inaudible macabre rhythm. Guided by some invisible puppeteers, the weapons suddenly turned towards him menacingly.

"Ohhh!" gasped Bari King as the weapons flew towards him.

Panting heavily and swallowing hard, Bari King flashed a terror-stricken expression. His eyes were transfixed on the weapons as they bobbed up and down in midair, few inches away from his heart.

A cacophonous laughter rang out and failed to distract his attention from the ominous weapons. An oppressive buzzing sound made its entrant and became an unholy accompaniment to the incredibly fast swirling motions of the weapons. Bari King trembled uncontrollably, and his dazed expression mirrored his utterly terrorized state. His fear did not abate as the weapons abruptly became still once more. Without warning, they drifted backwards in a bid to gather momentum for a strike. and Bari King held his breath. Posturing the palm of his hands defensively in front of his face, he still failed to bridle their trembling motions.

"Will you now acknowledge and bow to the lord and master of this realm?" thundered a malodorous voice.

Blinking nervously, Bari King resisted the urge to turn around and uncover the character behind the voice.

"You fate will be unbelievably tortuous if you continue to resist," boomed the voice.

All of a sudden, anger rose up within his consciousness and motivated him to challenge the oppressive bent of the voice. A defiant expression gradually supplanted the fear. He squinted his eyes as he mentally attempted to expunge traces of fear that were entangled in his consciousness.

A deafening hissing sound abruptly set upon him and hurled bestowals of discomfiture at him. Recoiling helplessly, he felt his fear, as it courageously staged a comeback. The weapons, suspended few inches away from his heart, by some unseen force, suddenly shifted backwards menacing. He closed his eyes and waited for their impact with great trepidation.

"Ha! ha! ha! ha!" came a very guttural voice, "We'll see how tough you are," it added.

Fear gripped him tightly and prevented him from opening his eyes. He struggled to restructure his mental poise and eloquence.

The commotion of sounds suddenly died down but suspicious thoughts still held sway inside his mind. Opening his eyes carefully, he encountered the familiar mass of desolate humanity and the bleak atmosphere of the realm. He sensed loneliness in a very intense manner and yearned to let go of it. He failed to uncover any other character that may be behind the oppressive episodes. Cautiously and as far as the dark grey atmosphere would permit; he peered into the distance in search of any suspicious object or being. The knowingness that peace would continue to elude him in the dark realm became an additional weight on his hung down head.

"He did I get here, and how can I escape this luckless realm?" he reflected, shaking his head despondently.

He thought of Agila and wondered why he abandoned him. The words of the jaguar man continued to ring inside his consciousness.

"I wonder what he meant when he stated that only I could save myself," he continued to ruminate.

As he lifted up his head, he beheld a very shapely and naked woman, as she waltzed towards him. His jaws dropped in bewilderment, when he realized that the woman mirrored Nengi's likeness.

"How's that possible, and what is this place?" he thought with furrowed temple.

The woman smiled coquettishly at him and continued to

narrow the distance that separated them. His wariness got the better of him, and he combated the urge to call her by name. The unemotional airs that radiated from her enlivened his apprehension.

In an instant and without any forewarning, the nude woman transformed into the dark monster that ruled the realm. The spectacle froze Bari King's motions in entirety, and even his breathing motions were guided with extreme caution.

"I got your juices running there, didn't I? ha! ha! ha! ha! ha!" muttered the monster with a gleeful smile, "you can't even imagine the boundaries of my power," he vaunted in a gruff tone, as he continued to advance towards him.

As the monster's grin turned into a nasty scowl, Bari King prevailed on his imagination to desist from conjuring further oppressive and frightening images.

"Grrrrr! What shall I do with you?" postured the entity, as its eyes mirrored maleficent intentions. With lightening speed, he grabbed Bari King by the neck. He suspended him in midair and vigorously shook him like a rag doll. Still in its oppressive clutches, he gasped for breath.

"Who's going to save you?" taunted the entity, tightening its grip around his neck.

Bravely, he struggled to unclasp the monster's rough hands, but he was no match for the brute force exhibited by it.

"Ha! Ha! Ha! You think you're tough, because you led a ragtag army while you sojourned on Earth; you are nothing but a minute organism I can easily squash; misery will continue to open the pages of your experiences here until you acknowledge me as your lord and Boss and bow before me," threatened the dark being.

Its suffocating foul breath blasted against his face and intensified his agony.

"Heeehu! heee heee!" gasped Bari King with a contorted expression.

An evil expression slithered across the entity's bloodshot eyes and mocked his helpless motions.

In a flash, the entity smashed him brutally on the bleak terrain. Towering above him in an exultant stance, it dared him with sheer body language. Cowering in a fetal position, he felt his thoughts as they ran amok. As Bari King shielded his head defensively, the shadow of the dark entity haunted his imagination.

"Are you ready now?" postured the entity, with eyes that mirrored victorious feelings.

"Never!" voiced Bari King vehemently, surprised at his courage.

"Grrrrrh!" raged the entity with eyes craz

ed by anger. Leaning towards Bari King, it mustered some unseen force and flung Bari King upwards, without laying its hands on him. With a satisfied grin, he viewed Bari King, as he tumbled towards the ground. Suspended in midair once more, he exhibited a dazed countenance. The crooked grin on the entity's face widened, as it observed his discomfiture. With brute force, he suddenly banged him against the ground.

"Ahhh!" gasped Bari King, as pin pricks of pain scared every part of his being.

"What do you say now," taunted the monster gruffly.

"Nothing!" asserted Bari King through grating teeth; "I will never bow to you even if you have the power to kill me," he continued.

"Kill! Who said anything about killing?" ejaculated the entity amusingly, "in this place, there is nothing like death"; it is pain and more pain, if you persist in your stubbornness," continued the monster ominously.

Emboldening his courage to override his fear, he continued to gaze defiantly at the monster.

"I see you have not learnt your lesson," hissed the entity.

He noticed that the fury, flaunted by the entity's eyes, was laced with strands of doubt. Energized by this knowingness, he reinforced his determination to resist till the end. Rush of vitality, attending to his resolve, continued to seep into his entire being. Suddenly, the monstrous being dematerialized; and bracing himself, Bari King prepared for the next onslaught.

A whooshing sound suddenly ensnared his attention. Turning towards its direction, he beheld a multitude of grotesque and dark serpents hurtling towards him, in midair. Fear reared its head inside his mind but his composed bodily motions betrayed his desire to stand his ground and hold on to his convictions. Stopping few inches away from him, the massed serpents bared their fangs and threatened him with deep guttural sounds. In a bid to defy his fear, he clenched his fists and glared at the serpents. The serpents bobbed up and down in midair and flashed their bloodshot eyes hatefully at him. The lead serpent drew closer to him and glowered at hm. The unrelenting rebellious glint in Bari King's eyes failed to trigger heightened aggressive behaviour from it. Without any sign, the massed serpents suddenly disappeared. His attention strayed to the bleak landscape and the self absorption of the doleful humanity.

"This is the last chance I will give you to salvage yourself in this realm, hrr! hrr! hrr," ejaculated the monster as it suddenly reappeared once more.

Startled out of his wits, Bari King veered towards it. The set determination in his eyes was unyielding, as he confronted the entity.

"You must serve me in order to survive here; there's no other way; I can give you real power you know, greater than the one you enjoyed on earth while you were the Boss," continued the dark being with grating gruffness.

Some semblance of pain pinched him at his sides, and he continued to safeguard his determination from being dampened by the bleak landscape. Bravely, he engaged the entity's eyes. A hint of indecision suddenly flashed in the inner recess of the monster's eyes before it abruptly dematerialized before him.

An ardent yearning for peace and a loving atmosphere swiftly swept through his entire being. He utterly submerged himself in the feelings of expansiveness that came in the wake of his yearning. His lightness of spirit led him to believe that some dross was being washed away from him.

A pinpoint of light suddenly loomed before him and began to expand. It transformed into a luminous male being. The visitor's eyes shone with an intense radiance that engendered an overpowering sense of wellbeing within Bari King. He wore a white tunic with a golden sash about his waist. Radiant golden light surrounded him and tempted Bari King to drown in it.

"Where did you come from?" queried Bari King lightheartedly, still displaying the gladness that heralded the advent of the light being.

"We have been here all along but your preoccupation with your hopelessness prevented you from seeing us; you only saw me, when your thoughts and desires aligned with us," projected the being of light telepathically.

Rapidly, Bari King turned about the dark grey realm and discovered numerous pinpoints of light. He instantly knew that they were other beings of light. As his attention rested on the mass of woebegone humanity that populated the realm, he was puzzled by their inability to detect the inimitable presence of the light beings. Swerving towards the being of light, he viewed his outstretched hand. The non-judgmental acceptance and understanding that flowed from the light being nurtured him with matchless sweetness. Without a second thought, he keenly reached out to him. Instantly, Bari King began to feel a familiar heaviness. He opened his eyes and realized that he was back in his physical body. Surveying the familiar bamboo members of the wall, his attention finally rested on Agila, who was propped up against the wall of the thatched hut in the forest.

"Welcome back!" voiced Agila with a broad smile.

Absentmindedly, he smiled at Agila. His attention still dwelt on his encounters with the light being, and the incomparable uplifting feelings he inspired inside him. He rued his departure and mentally struggled to hold on to his beatific feelings.

"That was quite some experience," stated Bari King, rising up and stretching himself.